FOR YOUR EYES ONLY/IAN FL

THUNDERBALL/IAN FLE

THE SPY WHO LOVED ME/IAN FLEM

ON HER MAJESTY'S SECRET SERVICE/FL

OU ONLY LIVE TWICE/FLEMI

HE MAN WITH THE GOLDEN GUN/FL

OCTOPUSSY/IAN FLEMING

'MY NAME'S BOND . . .'

'MY NAME'S

THE SPY WHO LOVED ME/IAN FLEMING

ON HER MAJESTY'S SECRET SERVICE/FLEMING

YOU ONLY LIVE TWICE/FLEMING

THE MAN WITH THE GOLDEN GUN/FLEMING

OCTOPUSSY/IAN FLEMING

BOND . . .'

an anthology
from the fiction of
IAN FLEMING

Edited by Simon Winder

ALLEN LANE
THE PENGUIN PRESS

ALLEN LANE
THE PENGUIN PRESS

Published by the Penguin Group
Penguin Books Ltd, 27 Wrights Lane, London w8 5tz, England
Penguin Putnam Inc., 375 Hudson Street, New York, New York 10014, USA
Penguin Books Australia Ltd, Ringwood, Victoria, Australia
Penguin Books Canada Ltd, 10 Alcorn Avenue, Toronto, Ontario, Canada m4v 3b2
Penguin Books (NZ) Ltd, Private Bag 102902, NSMC, Auckland, New Zealand
Penguin Books Ltd, Registered Offices: Harmondsworth, Middlesex, England

This anthology first published 2000
2

Set in 11/15.25 pt PostScript Adobe Caslon
Printed and bound by Omnia Books Ltd, Scotland

A CIP catalogue record for this book is available from the British Library

ISBN 0-713-99475-4

For AB

CONTENTS

IAN FLEMING
(1908-1964)

PREFACE

This book has no grander aim than to celebrate Ian Fleming's novels. It is a clear-cut public good to have all the megalomaniac speeches, most of Bond's meals and Blofeld's Garden of Death in one convenient volume.

So much has been written about James Bond's cultural influence that I am saved from having to repeat such insights here. It is surely enough to say that Fleming's hold on the British male imagination remains so great that the landscape of our postwar culture would be unrecognizable without his iconic hero. He has nourished the fantasies of millions on a scale only otherwise approached by Tolkien – the other great literary maverick of the 1950s – and this stature makes him both oddly taken for granted and particularly worth celebrating.

Of course the books are often absurd or offensive or cheerfully self-parodic and this is I hope adequately honoured here, but they are also spectacularly written and have an imaginative excess which makes Fleming a quite exceptional writer. Later imitators have obscured the ceaseless originality and euphoria of the Bond novels. 'My Name's Bond . . .' puts these back at the centre of our concerns.

This is a book for fans – to me and for thousands of similar unfortunates there is an absolute value to many of the sentences in this book opaque to those who enjoy more nourishing pastimes. In this spirit the source of each quote has been removed and put in a key at the back to allow a harmless quiz element. Many quotes have self-evident sources, but some are of an obscurity that should challenge even the best-informed.

Many treasured scenes have not been included to avoid pointlessly spoiling plots – no villains are dispatched or final twists given away. As these are some of the books' finest moments there is cause for regret, but the material is so rich anyway that only rarely is a *real* loss felt (Bond's magical last encounter with Wint and Kidd; Scaramanga in his foetid swamp . . .).

One of the happy spin-offs of producing this book has been the endless dispute with friends over the individual novels' merits. The best argument for this anthology is that it reminds the reader of the many spectacular moments trapped in each book – Bond's first encounter with a barracuda in *Thunderball*, the greedy meal with M in *Moonraker*, Oddjob's home improvements in *Goldfinger* . . . None of the books is a perfectly satisfactory work of art – Fleming was cruelly aware of this and his impatience and ennui meant that even in the greatest of the books he ultimately goes off the boil. In *Dr No*, Fleming lavished immense care on delineating his foul villain and marvellous lair, but the reader can almost sense in the prose Fleming grimly typing up the unconvincing crimes that actually pay for the Doctor's lavish lifestyle. In a formal sense this is a shame, but it is also all of a piece. These lapses of concentration must go with the manic energy, the grand, sadistic set-pieces, the restless travelling, the compulsive fascination with *objects* that are the books' and the author's great claim to originality. Fleming is a unique figure in British literature and I hope that *'My Name's Bond . . .'* gives some sense of this.

Simon Winder

Many thanks to the Fleming estate and to Corinne Turner and Peter Janson-Smith for allowing this book's existence and to Pan Macmillan for the right to reproduce the classic Pan 1960s covers.

'007's here, sir.'

'Send him in,' said the metallic voice, and the red light of privacy went on above the door.

THE MAN

He was good-looking in a dark, rather cruel way

First name: JAMES. Height: 183 centimetres; weight: 76 kilograms; slim build; eyes: blue; hair: black; scar down right cheek and on left shoulder; signs of plastic surgery on back of right hand (see Appendix 'A'); all-round athlete; expert pistol shot, boxer, knife-thrower; does not use disguises. Languages: French and German. Smokes heavily (NB: special cigarettes with three gold bands); vices: drink, but not to excess, and women. Not thought to accept bribes . . .

This man is invariably armed with a .25 Beretta automatic pistol carried in a holster under his left arm. Magazine holds eight rounds. Has been known to carry a knife strapped to his left forearm; has used steel-capped shoes; knows the basic holds of judo. In general, fights with tenacity and has a high tolerance of pain (see Appendix 'B').

'This case isn't ripe yet. Until it is, our policy with Mr Big is to "live and let live".'

Bond looked quizzically at Captain Dexter.

'In my job,' he said, 'when I come up against a man like this one, I have another motto. It's "live and let die".'

As he tied his thin, double-ended, black satin tie, he paused for a moment and examined himself levelly in the mirror. His grey-blue eyes looked calmly back with a hint of ironical inquiry and the short lock of black hair which would never stay in place slowly subsided to form a thick comma above the right eyebrow. With the thin vertical scar down his right cheek the general effect was faintly piratical.

He was good-looking in a dark, rather cruel way and a scar showed whitely down his left cheek. I quickly put my hand up to hide my nakedness. Then he smiled and suddenly I thought I might be all right.

When he spoke my heart leaped. He was English!

Sluggsy said contemptuously, 'Kerist! A limey!'

Griffon Or broke in excitedly, 'And this charming motto of the line, "The World is Not Enough". You do not wish to have the right to it?'

'It is an excellent motto which I shall certainly adopt,' said Bond curtly.

The train was slowing down. They slid past sidings full of empty freight cars bearing names from all over the States – 'Lackawanna', 'Chesapeake and Ohio', 'Lehigh Valley', 'Seaboard Fruit Express', and the lilting 'Acheson, Topeka and Santa Fe' – names that held all the romance of the American railroads.

'British Railways?' thought Bond. He sighed . . .

He let go of me and thrust his gun up into its holster. He smelled of cordite and sweat. It was delicious. I reached up and kissed him.

Bond always distrusted short men. They grew up from childhood with an inferiority complex. All their lives they would strive to be big – bigger than the others who had teased them as a child. Napoleon had been short, and Hitler. It was the short men that had caused all the trouble in the world.

Now the grey-blue eyes looked back at him from the tanned face with the brilliant glint of suppressed excitement and accurate focus of the old days. He smiled ironically back at the introspective scrutiny that so many people make of themselves before a race, a contest of wits, a trial of some sort. He had no excuses. He was ready to go.

Finally, after much crossing out and rewriting he said, 'Tiger, how's this? It makes just as much sense as old Basho and it's much more pithy.' He read out:
    'You only live twice:
    Once when you are born
    And once when you look death in the face.'
Tiger clapped his hands softly. He said with real delight, 'But that is excellent Bondo-san. Most sincere.'

In his imagination he could already hear the deep bark of the [rifle]. He could see the black bullet lazily, like a slow flying bee, homing down into the valley towards a square of pink skin. There was a light smack as it hit. The skin dented, broke and then closed up again, leaving a small hole with bruised edges. The bullet ploughed on, unhurriedly, towards the pulsing heart – the tissues, the blood-vessels, parting obediently to let it through. Who was this man he was going to do this to?

He had disobeyed many orders in his life, but this was to disobey the Prime Minister of England and the President of the United States – a mighty left and right.

Bond looked grimly at the pile of parcels which contained his new identity, stripped off his pyjamas for the last time ('We mostly sleep in the raw in America, Mr Bond') and gave himself a sizzling cold shower. The thick comma of black hair above his right eyebrow had lost some of its tail and his hair was trimmed close to the temples. Nothing could be done about the thin vertical scar down his right cheek.

. . . Naked, Bond walked out into the lobby . . .

He liked the solid, studied comfort of card-rooms and casinos, the well-padded arms of the chairs, the glass of champagne or whisky at the elbow, the quiet unhurried attention of good servants.

It was six o'clock on Thursday evening and Bond was packing his suitcase in his bedroom at the Ritz. It was a battered but once expensive pigskin Revelation and its contents were appropriate to his cover. Evening clothes; his lightweight black and white dog-tooth suit for the country and for golf; Saxone golf shoes; a companion to the dark blue, tropical worsted suit he was wearing, and some white silk and dark blue Sea Island cotton shirts with collars attached and short sleeves. Socks and ties, some nylon underclothes, and two pairs of the long silk pyjama coats he wore in place of two-piece pyjamas.

None of these things bore, or had ever borne, any name-tags or initials.

Bond completed his task and proceeded to fit his remaining possessions, his shaving and washing gear, Tommy Armour on *How to Play your Best Golf all the Time*, and his tickets and passport into a small attaché case, also of battered pigskin. This had been prepared for him by Q Branch and there was a narrow compartment under the leather at the back which contained a silencer for his gun and thirty rounds of .25 ammunition.

I mustn't let him go! But I knew in my heart that I had to. He would go on alone and I would have to, too. No woman had ever held this man. None ever would. He was a solitary, a man who walked alone and kept his heart to himself. He would hate involvement. I sighed.

The English word to be avoided at all costs, added Leiter, was 'Ectually'. Bond had said that this word was not part of his vocabulary.

It was typical of the cheap self-assertiveness of young labour since the war. This youth, thought Bond, makes about twenty pounds a week, despises his parents, and would like to be Tommy Steele. It's not his fault. He was born into the buyer's market of the Welfare State and into the age of atomic bombs and space flight. For him life is easy and meaningless.

Bond had always disliked pyjamas and had slept naked until in Hong Kong at the end of the war he came across the perfect compromise. This was a pyjama-coat which came almost down to the knees. It had no buttons, but there was a loose belt round the waist. The sleeves were wide and short, ending just above the elbow. The result was cool and comfortable and now when he slipped the coat on over his trunks, all his bruises and scars were hidden except the thin white bracelets on wrists and ankles and the mark of SMERSH on his right hand.

James Bond's choice of reading matter, prompted by a spectacular jacket of a half-naked girl strapped to a bed, turned out to have been a happy one for the occasion. It was called *Verderbt, Verdammt, Verraten.* The prefix 'ver' signified that the girl had not only been ruined, damned and betrayed, but that she had suffered these misfortunes most thoroughly. James Bond temporarily lost himself in the tribulations of the heroine, Gräfin Liselotte Mutzenbacher . . .

It was the beginning of a typical routine day for Bond. It was only two or three times a year that an assignment came along requiring his particular abilities. For the rest of the year he had the duties of an easy-going senior civil servant – elastic office hours from around ten to six; lunch, generally in the canteen; evenings spent playing cards in the company of a few close friends, or at Crockford's; or making love, with rather cold passion, to one of three similarly disposed married women; weekends playing golf for high stakes at one of the clubs near London.

He took no holidays, but was generally given a fortnight's leave at the end of each assignment – in addition to any sick-leave that might be necessary. He earned £1500 a year, the salary of a Principal Officer in the Civil Service, and he had a thousand a year free of tax of his own. When he was on a job he could spend as much as he liked, so for the other months of the year he could live very well on his £2000 a year net.

Was his personality changing? was he losing his edge, his point, his identity? Was he losing the vices that were so much a part of his ruthless, cruel, fundamentally tough character? Who was he in the process of becoming? A soft, dreaming, kindly idealist who would naturally leave the Service and become instead a prison visitor, interest himself in youth clubs, march with the H-bomb marchers, eat nut cutlets, try and change the world for the better?

Bond cursed into the sodden folds of his silk handkerchief and got going.

James Bond surveyed the glittering diamonds that lay scattered across the leather surface of M's desk and wondered what it was all about.

The quiet grey eyes were watching him thoughtfully.

Then M took the pipe out of his mouth and drily gave Bond details of the assignment of which even M was afraid.

And Bond walked out of the Headquarters of the Secret Service and into his greatest adventure.

supersonic John Buchan
LISTENER

the best thriller of the season
BIRMINGHAM POST

IAN FLEMING
Photo: Cecil Beaton

M
The frosty, damnably clear, grey eyes

'And you'd marry this person if you found her?'

'Not necessarily,' said Bond. 'Matter of fact I'm almost married already. To a man. Name begins with M. I'd have to divorce him before I tried to marry a woman. And I'm not sure I'd want that.'

M gestured to the chair opposite him across the red leather desk. Bond sat down and looked across into the tranquil, lined sailor's face that he loved, honoured and obeyed.

M: 'Doesn't do to get mixed up with neurotic women in this business. They hang on your gun-arm, if you know what I mean.'

There was the rasp of a match against a box and Bond watched M tamp the burning tobacco down in the bowl of his pipe and then put the matchbox back in his pocket and tilt his chair in M's favourite attitude for reflection.

M had one of the stock bachelor's hobbies. He painted in water-colour. He painted only the wild orchids of England, in the meticulous but uninspired fashion of the naturalists of the nineteenth century. He was now at his painting-table up against the window, his broad back hunched over his drawing-board, with, in front of him, an extremely dim little flower in a tooth-glass full of water.

It seemed to Bond that there was an extra small cleft of worry between the frosty, damnably clear, grey eyes.

Bond said: 'These people can't be hung, sir. But they ought to be killed . . .'

M opened the pad, tamped the rubber stamp on it and then carefully, so that it was properly aligned with the top right-hand corner of the docket, pressed it down on the grey cover.

M replaced the stamp and the ink pad in the drawer and closed the drawer. He turned the docket round and pushed it gently across the desk to Bond.

The red sans serif letters, still damp, said: FOR YOUR EYES ONLY.

Bond said nothing. He nodded and picked up the docket and walked out of the room.

At Blades, M ate his usual meagre luncheon – a grilled Dover sole followed by the ripest spoonful he could gouge from the club Stilton.

'I don't need a lecture on the qualities of the Swiss, thank you, 007. At least they keep their trains clean and cope with the beatnik problem.'

M looked morosely at Bond . . . 'People start preserving something – churches, old houses, decaying pictures, birds – and there's always a hullabaloo of some sort. The trouble is these people get really worked up about their damned birds or whatever it is. They get the politicians involved. And somehow they all seem to have stacks of money. God knows where it comes from. Other old women, I suppose . . .'

'Yes?' said the cold voice that Bond loved and obeyed.

'Humph.' M had never approved of Bond's womanizing.

[reading from the Scaramanga file] 'Now it may only be a myth, and it is certainly not medical science, but there is a popular theory that a man who cannot whistle has homosexual tendencies . . .' (M hadn't whistled since he was a boy. Unconsciously his mouth pursed and a clear note was emitted.)

[**M**] screwed up his eyes without humour. 'Hope the colour won't last too long. Always suspicious of sunburned men in England. Either they've not got a job of work to do or they put it on with a sun-lamp'. He dismissed the subject with a short sideways jerk of his pipe.

M lifted his eyes from his pipe and cleared his throat.

'Got anything particular on at the moment, James?' he asked in a neutral voice.

'James.' That was unusual. It was rare for M to use a Christian name in this room.

M looked like any member of any of the clubs in St James's Street. Dark grey suit, stiff white collar, the favourite dark blue bow-tie with spots, rather loosely tied, the thin black cord of the rimless eyeglass that M seemed only to use to read menus, the keen sailor's face, with the clear, sharp sailor's eyes. It was difficult to believe that an hour before he had been playing with a thousand live chessmen against the enemies of England; that there might be, this evening, fresh blood on his hands, or a successful burglary, or the hideous knowledge of a disgusting blackmail case.

M came over and sat heavily down in the chair and looked across at Bond. There was nothing to read in the lined sailor's face. It was as impassive as the polished blue leather of the empty chairback had been . . .

M reached for his in-basket and took out a file of signals. Without looking up he said: 'Look after yourself.'

M put both hands flat on the table. It was the old gesture when he came to the sixty-four-dollar question, and Bond's heart lifted even further at the sight of it. 'There's a man in Tokyo called Tiger Tanaka. Head of their Secret Service. Can't remember what they call it. Some unpronounceable Japanese rubbish . . .'

There was a creak from M's chair and Bond looked across the table at the man who held a great deal of his affection and all his loyalty and obedience.

'**A**ll drugs are harmful to the system. They are contrary to nature. The same applies to most of the food we eat – white bread with all the roughage removed, refined sugar with all the goodness machined out of it, pasteurized milk which has most of the vitamins boiled away, everything overcooked and denaturized. Why,' M reached into his pocket for his notebook and consulted it, 'do you know what our bread contains apart from a bit of overground flour?' M looked accusingly at Bond, 'It contains large quantities of chalk, also benzol peroxide powder, chlorine gas, sal ammoniac, and alum.' M put the notebook back in his pocket. 'What do you think of that?'

Bond, mystified by all this, said defensively, 'I don't eat all that much bread, sir.'

MASTERMINDS

*The scale of a Caligula,
of a Nero, of a Hitler . . .*

'You are indeed a genius, *lieber* Ernst. You have already established this place as a shrine to death for evermore. People read about such fantasies in the works of Poe, Lautreamont, de Sade, but no one has ever created such a fantasy in real life. It is as if one of the great fairy tales has come to life. A sort of Disneyland of Death. But of course,' she hastened to add, 'on an altogether grander, more poetic scale.'

'In due course I shall write the whole story down [replied Blofeld]. Then perhaps the world will acknowledge the type of man who has been living among them. A man not only unhonoured and unsung, but a man' – Blofeld's voice rose almost to a scream – 'whom they hunt down and wish to shoot like a mad dog.'

The very name of the organization was abhorred and avoided. SMERSH, 'Smiert Spionam', 'Death to Spies'. It was an obscene word, a word from the tomb, the very whisper of death, a word never mentioned even in secret office gossip among friends. Worst of all, within this horrible organization, Otdyel II, the Department of Torture and Death, was the central horror.

And the Head of Otdyel II, the woman, Rosa Klebb!

Doctor No said, in the same soft resonant voice, 'You are right, Mister Bond. That is just what I am, a maniac. All the greatest men are maniacs. They are possessed by a mania which drives them forward towards their goal. The great scientists, the philosophers, the religious leaders – all maniacs.'

'**Y**ou have doubtless read Trotter's *Instincts of the Herd in War and Peace*, Mister Bond. Well, I am by nature and predilection a wolf and I live by a wolf's laws. Naturally the sheep describe such a person as a "criminal".'

Kronsteen sat motionless and erect [at the chess-table], as malevolently inscrutable as a parrot. His elbows were on the table and his big head rested on clenched fists that pressed into his cheeks, squashing the pursed lips into a pout of hauteur and disdain. Under the wide, bulging brow the rather slanting black eyes looked down with deadly calm on his winning board. But, behind the mask, the blood was throbbing in the dynamo of his brain, and a thick worm-like vein in his right temple pulsed at a beat of over ninety. He had sweated away a pound of weight in the last two hours and ten minutes, and the spectre of a false move still had one hand at his throat. But to Makharov, and to the spectators, he was still 'The Wizard of Ice' whose game had been compared to a man eating fish. First he stripped off the skin, then he picked out the bones, then he ate the fish.

'Mr Bond, all my life I have been in love. I have been in love with gold. I love its colour, its brilliance, its divine heaviness. I love the texture of gold, that soft sliminess that I have learnt to gauge so accurately by touch that I can estimate the fineness of a bar to within one carat. And I love the warm tang it exudes when I melt it down into a true golden syrup. But, above all, Mr Bond, I love the power that gold alone gives to its owner – the magic of controlling energy, exacting labour, fulfilling one's every wish and whim and, when need be, purchasing bodies, minds, even souls. Yes, Mr Bond, I have worked all my life for gold and, in return, gold has worked for me and for those enterprises that I have espoused. I ask you,' Goldfinger gazed earnestly at Bond, 'is there any other substance on earth that so rewards its owner?'

It was said that Rosa Klebb would let no torturing take place without her. There was a blood-spattered smock in her office, and a low camp-stool, and they said that when she was seen scurrying through the basement passages dressed in the smock and with the stool in her hand, the word would go round, and even the workers in SMERSH would hush their words and bend low over their papers – perhaps even cross their fingers in their pockets – until she was reported back in her room.

For, or so they whispered, she would take the camp-stool and draw it up close below the face of the man or woman that hung down over the edge of the interrogation table . . . And she would watch the eyes in the face a few inches away from her and breathe in the screams as if they were perfume.

Mr Big sat looking at him, his huge head resting against the back of the tall chair. He said nothing.

Bond at once realized that the photographs had conveyed nothing of this man, nothing of the power and the intellect which seemed to radiate from him, nothing of the oversize features.

It was a great football of a head, twice the normal size and very nearly round. The skin was grey-black, taut and shining like the face of a week-old corpse in the river. It was hairless, except for some grey-brown fluff above the ears. There were no eyebrows and no eyelashes and the eyes were extraordinarily far apart so that one could not focus on them both, but only on one at a time. Their gaze was very steady and penetrating. When they rested on something, they seemed to devour it, to encompass the whole of it. They bulged slightly and the irises were golden around black pupils which were now wide. They were animal eyes, not human, and they seemed to blaze.

The nose was wide without being particularly negroid. The nostrils did not gape at you. The lips were only slightly everted, but thick and dark. They opened only when the man spoke and then they opened wide and drew back from the teeth and the pale pink gums.

There were few wrinkles or creases on the face, but there were two deep clefts above the nose, the clefts of concentration. Above them the forehead bulged slightly before merging with the polished, hairless crown.

Curiously, there was nothing disproportionate about the monstrous head. It was carried on a wide, short neck supported by the shoulders of a giant. Bond knew from the records that he was six and a half foot tall and weighted twenty stone, and that little of it was fat. But the total impression was awe-inspiring, even terrifying, and Bond could imagine that so ghastly a misfit must have been bent since childhood on revenge against fate and against the world that hated him because it feared him.

Bond dropped his lighted cigarette and left it to smoulder on the carpet. His whole body tensed. He said, 'I suppose you know you're both mad as hatters.'

'So was Frederick the Great, so was Nietzsche, so was Van Gogh. We are in good, in illustrious company, Mister Bond. On the other hand, what are you? You are a common thug, a blunt instrument wielded by dolts in high places. Having done what you are told to do, out of some mistaken idea of duty or patriotism, you satisfy your brutish instincts with alcohol, nicotine and sex while waiting to be dispatched on the next misbegotten foray.'

She looked like a very sunburned female wardress. She had a square, brutal face with hard yellow eyes. Her smile was an oblong hole without humour or welcome, and there were sunburn blisters at the left corner of her mouth which she licked from time to time with the tip of a pale tongue . . . Her strong, short body was dressed in unbecomingly tight vorlage trousers topped by a grey wind-jacket ornamented over the left breast with a large red G, topped by a coronet. Irma la not so Douce, thought Bond.

'You can spare us the jokes,' said Bond roughly. 'Get on with your story, Kraut.'

Drax's eyes blazed momentarily. 'A Kraut. Yes, I am indeed a *Reichsdeutscher*' – the mouth beneath the red moustache savoured the fine word – 'and even England will soon agree that they have been licked by just one single German. And then perhaps they'll stop calling us Krauts – BY ORDER!'

There was a moment's silence in the room. Then Doctor No came within three steps of them and stopped. The wound in the tall face opened. 'Forgive me for not shaking hands with you,' the deep voice was flat and even. 'I am unable to.' Slowly the sleeves parted and opened. 'I have no hands.'

The two pairs of steel pincers came out on their gleaming stalks and were held up for inspection like the hands of a praying mantis. Then the two sleeves joined again.

General G looked up and waved to the nearest chair at the conference table. 'Good evening, Comrade.'

The squat face split into a sugary smile. 'Good evening, Comrade General.'

Bond examined the man minutely. He was about five feet four with a boxer's shoulders and hips, but a stomach that was going to fat. A mat of black hair covered his breasts and shoulder blades, and his arms and legs were thick with it. By contrast, there was not a hair on his face or head and his skull was a glittering whitish yellow with a deep dent at the back that might have been a wound or the scar of a trepanning. The bone structure of the face was that of the conventional Prussian officer – square, hard and thrusting – but the eyes under the naked brows were close-set and piggish, and the large mouth had hideous lips – thick and wet and crimson. He wore nothing but a strip of black material, hardly larger than an athletic support-belt, around his stomach, and a large gold wrist-watch on a gold bracelet.

'Mister Bond, I suffer from boredom. I am a prey to what the early Christians called "accidie", the deadly lethargy that envelops those who are sated, those who have no more desires. I am absolutely pre-eminent in my chosen profession, trusted by those who occasionally employ my talents, feared and instantly obeyed by those whom I myself employ. I have, literally, no more worlds to conquer within my chosen orbit . . .

'Each day, Mister Bond, I try and set myself still higher standards of subtlety and technical polish so that each of my proceedings may be a work of art, bearing my signature as clearly as the creations of, let us say, Benvenuto Cellini. I am content, for the time being, to be my only judge, but I sincerely believe, Mister Bond, that the approach to perfection which I am steadily achieving in my operations will ulti-mately win recognition in the history of our times.'

Mr Big paused. Bond saw that his great yellow eyes were wide, as if he saw visions. He's a raving megalomaniac, thought Bond. And all the more dangerous because of it. The fault in most criminal minds was that greed was their only impulse. A dedicated mind was quite another matter. This man was no gangster. He was a menace.

On board the yacht, No. 1 put down his night glasses, took a Charvet handkerchief out of the breast pocket of his white shark-skin jacket and dabbed gently at his forehead and temples. The musky scent of Schiaparelli's *Snuff* was reassuring . . .

'**H**e has a woman once a month. Jill told me this when she first took the job. He hypnotizes them. Then he – he paints them with gold.'

'Christ! Why?'

'I don't know. Jill told me he's mad about gold. I suppose he sort of thinks he's – that he's sort of possessing gold. You know – marrying it. He gets some Korean servant to paint them. The man has to leave their backbones unpainted. Jill couldn't explain that. I found out it's so they wouldn't die. If their bodies were completely covered with gold paint, the pores of the skin wouldn't be able to breathe. Then they'd die. Afterwards, they're washed down by the Korean with resin or something. Goldfinger gives them a thousand dollars and sends them away.'

Bond saw the dreadful Oddjob with his pot of gold paint, Goldfinger's eyes gloating over the glistening statue, the fierce possession.

Blofeld, in his gleaming chain armour and grotesquely spiked and winged helmet of steel, its visor closed, was something out of Wagner, or, because of the oriental style of his armour, a Japanese *kabuki* play. His armoured right hand rested easily on a long naked *samurai* sword while his left was hooked into the arm of his companion, a stumpy woman with the body and stride of a wardress. Her face was totally obscured by a hideous bee-keeper's hat of dark-green straw with a heavy pendent black veil reaching down over her shoulders. But there could be no doubt! Bond had seen that dumpy silhouette, now clothed in a plastic rainproof above tall rubber boots, too often in his dreams. That was her! That was Irma Bunt!

Still smiling (Bond was to get used to that thin smile) Doctor No came slowly out from behind the desk and moved towards them. He seemed to glide rather than take steps. His knees did not dent the matt, gun-metal sheen of his kimono and no shoes showed below the sweeping hem.

Bond's first impression was of thinness and erectness and height. Doctor No was at least six inches taller than Bond, but the straight immovable poise of his body made him seem still taller. The head also was elongated and tapered from a round, completely bald skull down to a sharp chin so that the impression was of a reversed raindrop – or rather oildrop, for the skin was of a deep almost translucent yellow.

It was impossible to tell Doctor No's age: as far as Bond could see, there were no lines on the face. It was odd to see a forehead as smooth as the top of the polished skull. Even the cavernous indrawn cheeks below the prominent cheekbones looked as smooth as fine ivory. There was something Dali-esque about the eyebrows, which were fine and black and sharply upswept as if they had been painted on as make-up for a conjurer. Below them, slanting jet black eyes stared out of the skull. They were without eyelashes. They looked like the mouths of two small revolvers, direct and unblinking and totally devoid of expression. The thin fine nose ended very close above a wide compressed wound of a mouth which, despite its almost permanent sketch of a smile, showed only cruelty and authority. The chin was indrawn towards the neck. Later Bond was to notice that it rarely moved more than slightly away from centre, giving the impression that the head and the vertebra were in one piece.

The bizarre, gliding figure looked like a giant venomous worm wrapped in grey tin-foil, and Bond would not have been surprised to see the rest of it trailing slimily along the carpet behind.

And now Ernst Blofeld ... gazed slowly around the faces of his twenty men, and looked for eyes that didn't squarely meet his. Blofeld's own eyes were deep black pools surrounded – totally surrounded, as Mussolini's were – by very clear whites. The doll-like effect of this unusual symmetry was enhanced by long silken black eyelashes that should have belonged to a woman. The gaze of these soft doll's eyes was totally relaxed and rarely held any expression stronger than a mild curiosity in the object of their focus. They conveyed a restful certitude in their owner and in their analysis of what they observed. To the innocent, they exuded confidence, a wonderful cocoon of confidence in which the observed one could rest and relax knowing that he was in comfortable, reliable hands. But they stripped the guilty or the false and made them feel transparent – as transparent as a fishbowl through whose sides Blofeld examined, with only the most casual curiosity, the few solid fish, the grains of truth, suspended in the void of deceit or attempted obscurity. Blofeld's gaze was a microscope, the window on the world of a superbly clear brain, with a focus that had been sharpened by thirty years of danger and of keeping just one step ahead of it, and of an inner self-assurance built up on a lifetime of success in whatever he had attempted.

The skin beneath the eyes that now slowly, mildly, surveyed his colleagues was unpouched. There was no sign of debauchery, illness or old age in the large, white, bland face under the square, wiry black crew-cut. The jawline, going to the appropriate middle-aged fat of authority, showed decision and independence. Only the mouth, under a heavy, squat nose, marred what might have been the face of a philosopher or a scientist. Proud and thin, like a badly healed wound, the compressed, dark lips, capable only of false, ugly smiles, suggested contempt, tyranny and cruelty ... For the rest, he didn't smoke or drink and he had never been known to sleep with a member of either sex.

The china of [Le Chiffre's] whites was now veined with red. It was like looking at two blackcurrants poached in blood. The rest of the wide face was yellowish except where a thick black stubble covered the moist skin. The upward edges of black coffee at the corners of the mouth gave his expression a false smile and the whole face was faintly striped by the light from the venetian blinds.

He lowered his voice: 'Now, about this evening. Just leave the talking to me. Be natural and don't be worried by Doctor No. He may be a bit mad.'

Drax's fist crashed down on the desk, 'Hitler was betrayed again by those swinish generals and the English and Americans were allowed to land in France.'

'Too bad,' said Bond drily.

'Yes, my dear Bond, it was indeed too bad.' Drax chose to ignore the irony.

'Yo kin go on in, Tee-Hee,' said the man in evening dress.

Tee-Hee knocked on a door facing them, opened it and led the way through.

In a high-backed chair, behind an expensive desk, Mr Big sat looking quietly at them.

'Good morning, Mister James Bond.' The voice was deep and soft. 'Sit down.'

'This man is a monster. You may laugh, Bondo-san, but this man is no less than a fiend in human form.'

'I have met many bad men in my time, Tiger, and generally they have been slightly mad. Is that the case in this instance?'

'Very much the reverse. The calculated ingenuity of this man, his understanding of the psychology of my people, show him to be a man of quite outstanding genius. In the opinion of our highest scholars and savants he is a scientific research worker and collector probably unique in the history of the world.'

'What does he collect?'

'He collects death.'

Largo's voice was polite, unemotional. He said, 'I have one very short and simple answer to your suggestion, No. 10.' The light glittered redly on the metal thumb that protruded from the big hand. The three bullets pumped so quickly into the face of the Russian that the three explosions, the three bright flashes, were almost one. No. 10 put up two feeble hands, palms forward, as if to catch any further bullets, gave a jerk forward with his stomach at the edge of the table and then crashed heavily backwards, in a splinter of chair wood, on to the floor.

The whole demoniac concept was on Blofeld's usual grand scale – the scale of a Caligula, of a Nero, of a Hitler, of any other great enemy of mankind.

When Goldfinger had stood up, the first thing that had struck Bond was that everything was out of proportion. Goldfinger was short, not more than five feet tall, and on top of the thick body and blunt, peasant legs, was set almost directly into the shoulders, a huge and it seemed exactly round head. It was as if Goldfinger had been put together with bits of other people's bodies. Nothing seemed to belong. Perhaps, Bond thought, it was to conceal his ugliness that Goldfinger made such a fetish of sunburn. Without the red-brown camouflage the pale body would be grotesque. The face, under the cliff of crew-cut carroty hair, was as startling, without being as ugly, as the body. It was moonshaped without being moonlike. The fore-head was fine and high and the thin sandy brows were level above the large light blue eyes fringed with pale lashes . . . To sum up, thought Bond, it was the face of a thinker, perhaps a scientist, who was ruth-less, sensual, stoical and tough. An odd combination.

'FRANCISCO (PACO) "PISTOLS" SCARAMANGA . . . has thus become something of a local myth and is known in his "ter-ritory" as "The Man with the Golden Gun" – a reference to his main weapon which is a gold-plated, long-barrelled, single-action Colt .45 . . . Distinguishing marks: a third nipple about two inches below his left breast . . . an insatiable but indiscriminate womanizer who invari-ably has sexual intercourse before a killing in the belief that it improves his "eye". (NB, a belief shared by many professional lawn tennis players, golfers, gun and rifle marksmen and others.)'

As Bond followed her into the dining-room, it was quite an effort to restrain his right shoe from giving Irma Bunt a really tremendous kick in her tight, bulging behind.

Le Chiffre looked incuriously at him, the whites of his eyes, which showed all around the irises, lending something impassive and doll-like to his gaze.

He slowly removed one thick hand from the table and slipped it into the pocket of his dinner-jacket. The hand came out holding a small metal cylinder with a cap which Le Chiffre unscrewed. He inserted the nozzle of the cylinder with an obscene deliberation, twice into each black nostril in turn, and luxuriously inhaled the benzedrine vapour.

The veins on Drax's face started to swell and suddenly he pounded on the desk and shouted across at them, looking with bulging eyes from one to the other. 'I loathe and despise you all. You swine! Useless, idle, decadent fools, hiding behind your bloody white cliffs while other people fight your battles. Too weak to defend your colonies, toadying to America with your hats in your hands. Stinking snobs who'll do anything for money. Hah!' He was triumphant. 'I knew that all I needed was money and the façade of a gentleman. Gentleman! *Pfui Teufel!*'

'Yes,' said Bond. He looked levelly at the great red face across the desk. 'It's a remarkable case-history. Galloping paranoia. Delusions of jealousy and persecution. Megalomaniac hatred and desire for revenge. Curiously enough,' he went on conversationally, 'it may have something to do with your teeth. Diastema they call it. Comes from sucking your thumb when you're a child. Yes. I expect that's what the psychologists will say when they get you into the lunatic asylum. "Ogre's teeth." Being bullied at school and so on. Extraordinary the effect it has on a child. Then Nazism helped to fan the flames and then came the crack on your ugly head. The crack you engineered yourself. I expect that settled it. From then on you were really mad. Same sort of thing as people who think they're God. Extraordinary what tenacity they have. Absolute fanatics. You're almost a genius. Lombroso would have been delighted with you. As it is you're just a mad dog that'll have to be shot. Or else you'll commit suicide. Paranoics generally do. Too bad. Sad business.' Bond paused and put all the scorn he could summon into his voice. 'And now let's get on with this farce, you great hairy-faced lunatic.'

It worked. With every word Drax's face had become more contorted with rage, his eyes were red with it, the sweat of fury was dripping off his jowls on to his shirt, the lips were drawn back from the gaping teeth and a string of saliva had crept out of his mouth and was hanging down from his chin. Now, at the last private-school insult that must have awoken God knows what stinging memories, he leapt up from his chair and lunged around the desk at Bond, his hairy fists flailing.

KILLERS
The sickly zoo-smell of Oddjob enveloped him

This embryo tail of golden down above the cleft of the buttocks – in a lover it would have been gay, exciting, but on this man it was somehow bestial ... She looked back up the fine body. Was her revulsion *only* physical? Was it the reddish colour of the sunburn on the naturally milk-white skin, the sort of roast meat look? Was it the texture of the skin itself, the deep, widely spaced pores in the satiny surface? The thickly scattered orange freckles on the shoulders? Or was it the sexuality of the man? The indifference of these splendid, insolently bulging muscles? Or was it spiritual – an animal instinct telling her that inside this wonderful body there was an evil person?

Where this man was deadly, the other was merely unpleasant – a short, moon-faced youth with wet, very pale blue eyes and fat wet lips. His skin was very white and he had that hideous disease of no hair – no eyebrows and no eyelashes, and none on a head that was polished as a billiard ball. I would have felt sorry for him if I hadn't been so frightened, particularly as he seemed to have a bad cold and began blowing his nose as soon as he got his oilskins off. Under them he wore a black leather windcheater, grubby trousers and those Mexican saddle-leather boots with straps that they wear in Texas. He looked a young monster, the sort that pulls wings off flies ...

The man was extremely handsome – a dark bronzed woman-killer with a neat moustache about the sort of callous mouth women kiss in their dreams. He had regular features that suggested Spanish or South American blood and bold, hard brown eyes that turned up oddly, or, as a woman would put it, intriguingly, at the corners. He was an athletic-looking six foot, dressed in the sort of casually well-cut beige herring-bone tweed that suggests Anderson and Sheppard. He wore a white silk shirt and a dark red polka-dot tie, and the soft dark brown V-necked sweater looked like vicuña. Bond summed him up as a good-looking bastard who got all the women he wanted and probably lived on them – and lived well.

He looked incuriously at Bond and his mouth was square with the empty letter-box smile. From the middle of his smile a wooden toothpick protruded from between closed teeth like the tongue of a snake.

[Sol] was tall and thin, almost skeletal, and his skin had this grey, drowned look as if he always lived indoors. The black eyes were slow-moving, incurious, and the lips thin and purplish like an unstitched wound. When he spoke there was a glint of grey silvery metal from his front teeth and I supposed they had been cheaply capped with steel, as I had heard was done in Russia and Japan. The ears lay very flat and close to the bony, rather box-shaped head and the stiff, greyish-black hair was cut so close to the skull that the skin showed whitely through it . . . He was a frightening lizard of a man, and my skin crawled with fear of him.

The one more or less behind Le Chiffre's right arm was tall and funereal in his dinner-jacket. His face was wooden and grey, but his eyes flickered and gleamed like a conjurer's. His whole long body was restless and his hands shifted on the brass rail. Bond guessed that he would kill without interest or concern for what he killed and that he would prefer strangling. He had something of Lennie in *Of Mice and Men*, but his inhumanity would not come from infantilism but from drugs. Marihuana, decided Bond.

The other man looked like a Corsican shopkeeper. He was short and very dark with a flat head covered with thickly greased hair. He seemed to be a cripple. A chunky malacca cane with a rubber tip hung on the rail beside him. He must have had permission to bring the cane into the Casino with him, reflected Bond, who knew that neither sticks nor any other objects were allowed in the rooms as a precaution against acts of violence. He looked sleek and well fed. His mouth hung vacantly half-open and revealed very bad teeth. He wore a heavy black moustache and the backs of his hands on the rail were matted with black hair. Bond guessed that hair covered most of his squat body. Naked, Bond supposed, he would be an obscene object.

Bond closed his eyes. The sickly zoo-smell of Oddjob enveloped him. Big, rasping fingers set to work on him carefully, delicately. A pressure here, combined with a pressure there, a sudden squeeze, a pause, and then a quick, sharp blow. Always the hard hands were surgically accurate. Bond ground his teeth until he thought they would break. The sweat of pain began to form pools in the sockets of his closed eyes.

He was a chunky flat-faced Japanese, or more probably Korean, with a wild, almost mad stare in dramatically slanted eyes that belonged in a Japanese film rather than in a Rolls-Royce on a sunny afternoon in Kent. He had the snout-like upper lip that sometimes goes with a cleft palate, but he said nothing and Bond had no opportunity of knowing whether his guess was right. In his tight, almost bursting black suit and farcical bowler hat he looked rather like a Japanese wrestler on his day off. But he was not a figure to make one smile. If one had been inclined to smile, a touch of the sinister, the unexplained, in the tight shining patent-leather black shoes that were almost dancing pumps, and in the heavy black leather driving gloves, would have changed one's mind.

A man with very bright red hair and a big peaceful moon-shaped face was sitting at a desk. There was a big glass of milk in front of him. He stood up as they came in and Bond saw he was a hunchback. Bond didn't remember having seen a red-haired hunchback before. He could imagine that the combination would be useful for frightening the small fry who worked for the gang . . . Bond looked impassively back into a pair of china eyes that were so empty and motionless that they might have been hired from a taxidermist. Bond had the feeling that he was being subjected to some sort of test. Casually he looked back at the hunchback, noting the big ears with rather exaggerated lobes, the dry red lips of the big half-open mouth, the almost complete absence of a neck, and the short powerful arms in the expensive yellow silk shirt, cut to make room for the barrel-like chest and its sharp hump.

As Strangways had passed the last man, all three had swivelled. The back two had fanned out a step to have a clear field of fire. Three revolvers, ungainly with their sausage-shaped silencers, whipped out of holsters concealed among the rags. With disciplined precision the three men aimed at different points down Strangways's spine – one between the shoulders, one in the small of the back, one at the pelvis.

The three heavy coughs were almost one. Strangways's body was hurled forward as if it had been kicked. It lay absolutely still in the small puff of dust from the sidewalk.

There was something cruel about the thin-lipped rather pursed mouth, a piggishness about the wide nostrils in the upturned nose, and the blankness that veiled the very pale blue eyes communicated itself over the whole face and made it look drowned and morgue-like. It was, she reflected, as if someone had taken a china doll and painted its face to frighten.

The two dead-pan, professional faces told him even more than the two silver eyes of the guns. They held no tension, no excitement. The thin half-smiles were relaxed, contented. The eyes were not even wary. They were almost bored. Bond had looked into such faces many times before. This was routine. These men were killers – pro-killers.

'**W**as there anything that struck you about these two guys?' asked Leiter. 'Height, clothes, anything else?'

'I couldn't see much of the man by the door,' said Bond. 'He was smaller than the other and thinner. Wearing dark trousers and a grey shirt with no tie. Gun looked like a .45. Might have been a Colt. The other man, the one who did the job, was a big, fattish guy. Quick moving but deliberate. Black trousers. Brown shirt with white stripes. No coat or tie. Black shoes, neat, expensive. .38 Police Positive. No wrist-watch. Oh, yes,' Bond suddenly remembered. 'He had a wart on the top joint of his right thumb. Red-looking as if he had sucked it.'

'Wint,' said Leiter flatly. 'And the other guy was Kidd. Always work together. They're the top torpedoes for the Spangs. Wint is a mean bastard. A real sadist. Likes it. He's always sucking at that wart on his thumb. He's called "Windy". Not to his face, that is. All these guys have crazy names. Wint can't bear to travel. Gets sick in cars and trains and thinks planes are death traps. Has to be paid a special bonus if there's a job that means moving around the country. But he's cool enough when his feet are on the ground. Kidd's a pretty boy. His friends call him "Boofy". Probably shacks up with Wint. Some of these homos make the worst killers. Kidd's got white hair although he's only thirty. That's one of the reasons they like to work in hoods. But one day that fellow Wint is going to be sorry he didn't have that wart burned away.'

Bond had no illusions about being able to beat this terrific man in unarmed combat. The first violent stab of the knife had to be decisive.

Bond's skin crawled minutely at this proximity to treachery and at the black and deadly secret locked up beneath the frilly white blouse. She was an unattractive girl with a pale, rather pimply skin, black hair and a vaguely unwashed appearance. Such a girl would be unloved, make few friends, have chips on her shoulder – more particularly in view of her illegitimacy – and a grouse against society. Perhaps her only pleasure in life was the triumphant secret she harboured in that flattish bosom – the knowledge that she was cleverer than all those around her, that she was, every day, hitting back against the world – the world that despised her, or just ignored her, because of her plainness – with all her might. One day they'd be sorry! It was a common neurotic pattern – the revenge of the ugly duckling on society.

On the door was a sign: 'Private. Keep Out.'

Against this a man sat on a kitchen chair, its back tilted so that the door supported his weight. He was cleaning a rifle, a Remington 30, it looked like to Bond. He had a wooden toothpick sticking out of his mouth and a battered baseball cap on the back of his head. He was wearing a stained white singlet that revealed tufts of black hair under his arms, and slept-in white canvas trousers and rubber-soled sneakers. He was around forty and his face was as knotted and seamed as the mooring posts on the jetty. It was a thin, hatchet face, and the lips were thin too, and bloodless. His complexion was the colour of tobacco dust, a sort of yellowy-beige. He looked cruel and cold, like the bad man in a film about poker-players and gold mines.

The thin man had hit him a hard professional cutting blow with the edge of the hand. There was something rather deadly about his accuracy and lack of effort. He was now again lying back, his eyes closed. He was a man to make you afraid, an evil man. Bond hoped he might get a chance of killing him.

'Seems the men you got were a pretty nasty trio – Tee-Hee Johnson, Sam Miami and a man called McThing.'

There was the touch of a slightly damp hand. 'Ferry pleased to meet you,' said an ingratiating voice and Bond looked into a pale round unhealthy face now split in a stage smile which died almost as Bond noticed it. Bond looked into his eyes. They were like two restless black buttons and they twisted away from Bond's gaze.

Krebs echoed the maniac laugh with a high giggle. 'A masterstroke, *mein Kapitän*. You should have seen them charge off down the hill. The one that burst. *Wunderschön!*'

Pissaro looked like a gangster in a horror comic. He had a round bladder-like head in the middle of which the features were crowded together – two pin-point eyes, two black nostrils, a pursed wet pink mouth above the hint of a chin, and a fat body in a brown suit and a white shirt with a long-pointed collar and a figured chocolate bow tie. He paid no attention to the preparations for the first race but concentrated on his food, occasionally glancing across at his companion's plate as if he might reach across and fork something off it for himself . . .

Pissaro picked his teeth until a mound of ice cream arrived, and then he bent his head again and started spooning the ice cream rapidly up into his small mouth.

And then, with a ripping noise high up on the opposite wall, the bits of curtain hung sideways. And a big, glittering turnip-face, pale and shiny under the moon, was looking through the glass slats!

Bond turned his head to the right. A few feet away stood the Korean. He still wore his bowler hat but now he was stripped to the waist. The yellow skin of his huge torso glinted with sweat. There was no hair on it. The flat pectoral muscles were as broad as dinner plates and the stomach was concave below the great arch of the ribs. The biceps and forearms, also hairless, were as thick as thighs. The ten-minutes-to-two oil slicks of the eyes looked pleased, greedy. The mouthful of blackish teeth formed an oblong grin of anticipation.

And one of the businessmen was youngish, with a pretty face and a glimpse of prematurely white hair under the Stetson with the waterproof cover, and the name on the briefcase he was carrying was B. Kitteridge.

And the other was a big, fattish man with a nervous glare in the small eyes behind the bi-focals, and he was sweating profusely and constantly wiped his face round with a big handkerchief.

And the name on the label of his grip was W. Winter and below the name, in red ink, was written: MY BLOOD GROUP IS F.

DR NO'S GIFT

[From *Dr No*. Bond is in his hotel room in Jamaica.]

He telephoned down and arranged to be called at five-thirty. Then he bolted the door on the inside, and also shut and bolted the slatted jalousies across the windows. It would mean a hot, stuffy night. That couldn't be helped. Bond climbed naked under the single cotton sheet and turned over on his left side and slipped his right hand on to the butt of the Walther PPK under the pillow. In five minutes he was asleep.

The next thing Bond knew was that it was three o'clock in the morning. He knew it was three o'clock because the luminous dial of his watch was close to his face. He lay absolutely still. There was not a sound in the room. He strained his ears. Outside, too, it was deathly quiet. Far in the distance a dog started to bark. Other dogs joined in and there was a brief hysterical chorus which stopped as suddenly as it had begun. Then it was quite quiet again. The moon coming through the slats in the jalousies threw black and white bars across the corner of the room next to his bed. It was as if he was lying in a cage. What had woken him up? Bond moved softly, preparing to slip out of bed.

Bond stopped moving. He stopped as dead as a live man can.

Something had stirred on his right ankle. Now it was moving up the inside of his shin. Bond could feel the hairs on his leg being parted. It was an insect of some sort. A very big one. It was long, five or six inches – as long as his hand. He could feel dozens of tiny feet lightly touching his skin. What was it?

Then Bond heard something he had never heard before – the sound of the hair on his head rasping up on the pillow. Bond analysed the noise. It couldn't be! It simply couldn't! Yes, his hair was standing on end. Bond could even feel the cool air reaching his scalp between the hairs. How extraordinary! How very extraordinary! He had always thought it was a figure of speech. But why? Why was it happening to him?

The thing on his leg moved. Suddenly Bond realized that he was afraid, terrified. His instincts, even before they had communicated with his brain, had told his body that he had a centipede on him.

Bond lay frozen. He had once seen a tropical centipede in a bottle of spirit on the shelf of a museum. It had been pale brown and very flat and five or six inches long – about the length of this one. On either side of the blunt head there had been curved poison claws. The label on the bottle had said that its poison was mortal if it hit an artery. Bond had looked curiously at the corkscrew of dead cuticle and had moved on.

The centipede had reached his knee. It was starting up his thigh. Whatever happened he mustn't move, mustn't even tremble. Bond's whole consciousness had drained down to the two rows of softly creeping feet. Now they had reached his flank. God, it was turning down towards his groin! Bond set his teeth! Supposing it liked the warmth there! Supposing it tried to crawl into the crevices! Could he stand it? Supposing it chose that place to bite? Bond could feel it questing amongst the first hairs. It tickled. The skin on Bond's belly fluttered. There was nothing he could do to control it. But now the thing was turning up and along his stomach. Its feet were gripping tighter to prevent it falling. Now it was at his heart. If it bit there, surely it would kill him. The centipede trampled steadily on through the thin hairs on Bond's right breast up to his collar bone. It stopped. What was it doing? Bond could feel the blunt head questing blindly to and fro. What was it looking for? Was there room between his skin and the sheet for it to get through? Dare he lift the sheet an inch to help it. No. Never! The animal was at the base of his jugular. Christ, if only he could control the pumping of his blood. Damn you! Bond tried to communicate with the centipede. It's nothing. It's not dangerous, that pulse. It means you no harm. Get on out into the fresh air!

As if the beast had heard, it moved on up the column of the neck and into the stubble on Bond's chin. Now it was at the corner of his mouth, tickling madly. On it went, up along the nose. Now he could feel its whole weight and length. Softly Bond closed his eyes. Two by two the pairs of feet moving alternately, trampled across his right eyelid. When it got off his eye, should he take a chance and shake it off – rely on its feet slipping in his sweat? No, for God's sake! The grip of the feet was endless. He might shake one lot off, but not the rest.

With incredible deliberation the huge insect ambled across Bond's forehead. It stopped below the hair. What the hell was it doing now? Bond could feel it nuzzling at his skin. It was drinking! Drinking the beads of salt sweat. Bond was sure of it. For minutes it hardly moved. Bond felt weak with the tension. He could feel the sweat pouring off the rest of his body on to the sheet. In a second his limbs would start to tremble. He could feel it coming on. He would start to shake with an ague of fear. Could he control it, could he? Bond lay and waited, the breath coming softly through his open, snarling mouth.

The centipede started to move again. It walked into the forest of hair. Bond could feel the roots being pushed aside as it forced its way along. Would it like it there? Would it settle down? How did centipedes sleep? Curled up, or at full length? The tiny centipedes he had known as a child, the ones that always seemed to find their way up the plughole into the empty bath, curled up when you touched them. Now it had come to where his head lay against the sheet. Would it walk out on to the pillow or would it stay on in the warm forest? The centipede stopped. Out! OUT! Bond's nerves screamed at it.

The centipede stirred. Slowly it walked out of his hair on to the pillow.

Bond waited a second. Now he could hear the rows of feet picking softly at the cotton. It was a tiny scraping noise, like soft fingernails.

With a crash that shook the room Bond's body jackknifed out of bed and onto the floor.

At once Bond was on his feet and at the door. He turned on the light. He found he was shaking uncontrollably. He staggered to the bed. There it was crawling out of sight over the edge of the pillow. Bond's first instinct was to twitch the pillow on to the floor. He controlled himself, waiting for his nerves to quieten. Then softly, deliberately, he picked up the pillow by one corner and walked into the middle of the room and dropped it. The centipede came out from under the pillow. It started to snake swiftly away across the matting. Now Bond was uninterested. He looked round for something to kill it with. Slowly he went and picked up a shoe and came back. The danger was past. His mind was now wondering how the centipede had got into his bed. He lifted the shoe and slowly, almost carelessly, smashed it down. He heard the crack of the hard carapace.

Bond lifted the shoe.

The centipede was whipping from side to side in its agony – five inches of grey-brown, shiny death. Bond hit it again. It burst open, yellowly.

Bond dropped the shoe and ran for the bathroom and was violently sick.

WEAPONS

A very flat .25 Beretta automatic with a skeleton grip

He reached under the dashboard and from its concealed holster drew out the long-barrelled .45 Colt Army Special and laid it on the seat beside him. The battle was now in the open and somehow the Mercedes had to be stopped.

Q Branch had put together this smart-looking little bag, ripping out the careful handiwork of Swaine and Adeney to pack fifty rounds of .25 ammunition, in two flat rows, between the leather and the line of the spine. In each of the innocent sides there was a flat throwing knife, built by Wilkinsons, the sword makers, and the tops of their handles were concealed cleverly by the stitching at the corners. Despite Bond's efforts to laugh them out of it, Q's craftsmen had insisted on building a hidden compartment into the handle of the case, which, by pressure at a certain point, would deliver a cyanide death-pill into the palm of his hand. (Directly he had taken delivery of the case, Bond had washed this pill down the lavatory.) More important was the thick tube of Palmolive shaving cream in the otherwise guileless sponge-bag. The whole top of this unscrewed to reveal the silencer for the Beretta, packed in cotton wool. In case hard cash was needed, the lid of the attaché case contained fifty golden sovereigns. These could be poured out by slipping sideways one ridge of welting.

Bond was then led into the castle to drink tea and view the museum of *ninja* armament. This included spiked steel wheels, the size of a silver dollar, which could be whirled on the finger and thrown, chains with spiked weights at each end, used like the South American bolas for catching cattle, sharp nails twisted into knots for defeating barefoot pursuers (Bond remembered similar devices spread on the roads by the Resistance to puncture the tyres of German staff cars), hollowed bamboo for breathing under water (Bond had used the same device during an adventure on a Caribbean island), varieties of brass knuckles, gloves whose palms were studded with very sharp, slightly hooked nails for 'walking' up walls and across ceilings, and a host of similar rather primitive gadgets of offence and defence. Bond made appropriate noises of approval and amazement . . .

After pocketing the thin sheaf of ten-mille notes, he opened a drawer and took out a light chamois leather holster and slipped it over his left shoulder so that it hung about three inches below his armpit. He then took from under his shirts in another drawer a very flat .25 Beretta automatic with a skeleton grip, extracting the clip and the single round in the barrel and whipped the action to and fro several times, finally pulling the trigger on the empty chamber. He charged the weapon again, loaded it, put up the safety catch and dropped it into the shallow pouch of the shoulder-holster.

When he was twenty yards away, Colombo said quietly: 'Put away your toy, Mr Bond of the Secret Service. These are CO_2 harpoon guns. And stay where you are. Unless you wish to make a copy of Mantegna's *St Sebastian*.' He turned to the man on his right. He spoke in English. 'At what range was that Albanian last week?'

'Twenty yards, padrone. And the harpoon went right through. But he was a fat man – perhaps twice as thick as this one.'

[**B**ond's] eyes, his mind, were barely in focus as he turned the pages of a jaw-breaking dissertation by the Scientific Research Section on the Russian use of cyanide gas, propelled by the cheapest bulb-handled children's water pistol, for assassination. The spray, it seemed, directed at the face, took instantaneous effect. It was recommended for victims from twenty-five years upwards, on ascending stairways or inclines. The verdict would then probably be heart failure.

'**K**alashnikov,' he said curtly. 'Sub-machine-gun. Gas-operated. Thirty rounds in 7.62 millimetre. Favourite with the KGB. They're going to do a saturation job after all. Perfect for the range. We'll have to get him pretty quick or 272'll end up not just dead but strawberry jam.'

'Anything else you'd like me to fix up?'

Bond had been making up his mind.

'Yes,' he said. 'You might ask London to get the Admiralty to lend us one of their frogman suits complete with compressed-air bottles. Plenty of spares. And a couple of good underwater harpoon guns. The French ones called "Champion" are the best. Good underwater torch. A commando dagger. All the dope they can get from the Natural History Museum on barracuda and shark. And some of that shark-repellent stuff the Americans used in the Pacific. Ask BOAC to fly it all out on their direct service.'

Bond paused. 'Oh yes,' he said. 'And one of those things our saboteurs used against ships in the war. Limpet mine, with assorted fuses.'

On an impulse, Bond went over to his bed and took the Walther from under the pillow. He slipped out the magazine and pumped the single round on to the counterpane. He tested the spring of the magazine and of the breech and drew a quick bead on various objects around the room. He found he was aiming an inch or so high. But that would be because the gun was lighter without its loaded magazine. He snapped the magazine back and tried again. Yes, that was better.

Bond went back to his suitcase again and took out a thick book – *The Bible Designed to be Read as Literature* – opened it and extracted his Walther PPK in the Berns Martin holster. He slipped the holster inside his trouser band to the left. He tried one or two quick draws. They were satisfactory.

He looked round the room. Everything was ready. On an impulse, he put his right hand under his coat and drew the .25 Beretta automatic with the skeleton grip out of the chamois leather holster that hung just below his left armpit. It was the new gun M had given him 'as a memento' after his last assignment, with a note in M's green ink that had said, *You may need this.*

Bond knelt to the drawers under the bunk and opened them. They contained all the contents of his suitcase except his watch and the gun. Even the rather heavy shoes he had been wearing on his expedition to Entreprises Auric were there. He twisted one of the heels and pulled. The broad double-sided knife slid smoothly out of its scabbard in the sole. With the fingers wrapped round the locked heel it made a workmanlike stabbing dagger.

There are hundreds of secret inks, but there was only one available to Bond, the oldest one in the world, his own urine.

'Morning, Armourer. Now I want to ask you some questions.' M's voice was casual. 'First of all, what do you think of the Beretta, the .25?'

'Ladies' gun, sir.'

M raised ironic eyebrows at Bond. Bond smiled thinly.

'Really! And why do you say that?'

'No stopping power, sir. But it's easy to operate. A bit fancy-looking too, if you know what I mean, sir. Appeals to the ladies . . . Might I see your gun?'

Bond's hand went slowly into his coat. He handed over the taped Beretta with the sawn barrel. Boothroyd examined the gun and weighed it in his hand. He put it down on the desk.

'And your holster?'

Bond took off his coat and slipped off the chamois leather holster and harness. He put his coat on again.

With a glance at the lips of the holster, perhaps to see if they showed traces of snagging, Boothroyd tossed the holster down beside the gun with a motion that sneered. He looked across at M. 'I think we can do better than this, sir.' It was the sort of voice Bond's first expensive tailor had used.

Bond sat down. He just stopped himself gazing rudely at the ceiling. Instead he looked impassively across at M.

'Well, Armourer, what do you recommend?'

Major Boothroyd put on the expert's voice. 'As a matter of fact, sir,' he said modestly, 'I've just been testing most of the small automatics. Five thousand rounds each at twenty-five yards. Of all of them, I'd choose the Walther PPK 7.65 mm. It only came fourth after the Japanese M-14, the Russian Tokarev and the Sauer M-38. But I like its light trigger pull and the extension spur of the magazine gives a grip that should suit 007. It's a real stopping gun. Of course it's about a .32 calibre as compared with the Beretta's .25 but I wouldn't recommend anything lighter. And you can get ammunition for the Walther anywhere in the world. That gives it an edge on the Japanese and the Russian guns.'

His eyes slid to the gun and holster on the desk. He remembered the times its single word had saved his life – and the times when its threat alone had been enough.

WOMEN
And who in heaven's name was Miss Pussy Galore?

With her hands clasped behind her back, gazing raptly upwards at the glittering fifty feet of the Moonraker, she might have been a schoolgirl looking up at a Christmas tree – except for the impudent pride of the jutting breasts, swept up by the thrown-back head and shoulders.

She was an athletic-looking girl whom Bond would have casually associated with tennis, or skating, or show-jumping. She had the sort of firm, compact figure that always attracted him and a fresh open-air type of prettiness that would have been commonplace but for a wide, rather passionate mouth and a hint of authority that would be a challenge to men. She was dressed in a feminine version of the white smock worn by Mr Wain, and it was clear from the undisguised curves of her breasts and hips that she had little on underneath it.

She held her body proudly – her fine breasts out-thrown and unashamed under the taut silk. Her stance, with feet slightly parted and hands behind her back, was a mixture of provocation and challenge.

Her face was pale, with the pallor of white families that have lived long in the tropics. But it contained no trace of the usual exhaustion which the tropics impart to the skin and hair. The eyes were blue, alight and disdainful, but, as they gazed into his with a touch of humour, he realized they contained some message for him personally. It quickly vanished as his own eyes answered. Her hair was blue-black and fell heavily to her shoulders. She had high cheekbones and a wide, sensual mouth which held a hint of cruelty. Her jawline was delicate and finely cut . . . Part of the beauty of the face lay in its lack of compromise. It was a face born to command. The face of the daughter of a French Colonial slave-owner . . .

Altogether, Bond decided, she was a very lovely girl and beneath her reserve, a very passionate one. And, he reflected, she might be a policewoman and an expert at jujitsu, but she also had a mole on her right breast.

Miss Moneypenny, M's private secretary, looked up from her typewriter and smiled at him. They liked each other and she knew that Bond admired her looks. She was wearing the same model shirt as his own secretary, but with blue stripes.

'New uniform, Penny?' said Bond.

She laughed. 'Loelia and I share the same little woman.'

She took his face between her two hands and held it away, panting. Her eyes were bright and hot. Then she brought his lips against hers again and kissed him long and lasciviously, as if she was the man and he the woman.

Bond cursed the broken hand that prevented him exploring her body, taking her. He freed his right hand and put it between their bodies, feeling her hard breasts, each with its pointed stigma of desire.

She stood up and took her hand away from her mouth. She was tall, perhaps five feet ten, and her arms and legs looked firm as if she might be a swimmer. Her breasts thrust against the silk of the brassière.

The photograph of her record-sheet at the Yard had shown an attractive but rather severe girl and any hint of seductiveness had been abstracted by the cheerless jacket of her policewoman's uniform.

Hair: Auburn. Eyes: Blue. Height: 5 ft 7. Weight: 9 stone. Hips: 38. Waist: 26. Bust: 38. Distinguishing marks: Mole on upper curvature of right breast.

Hm! thought Bond.

Bond sat down beside her. 'Tania,' he said, 'If there was a bit more room I'd put you across my knee and spank you.'

She was tall and dark with a reserved, unbroken beauty to which the war and five years in the Service had lent a touch of sternness. Unless she married soon, Bond thought for the hundredth time, or had a lover, her cool air of authority might easily become spinsterish and she would join the army of women who had married a career.

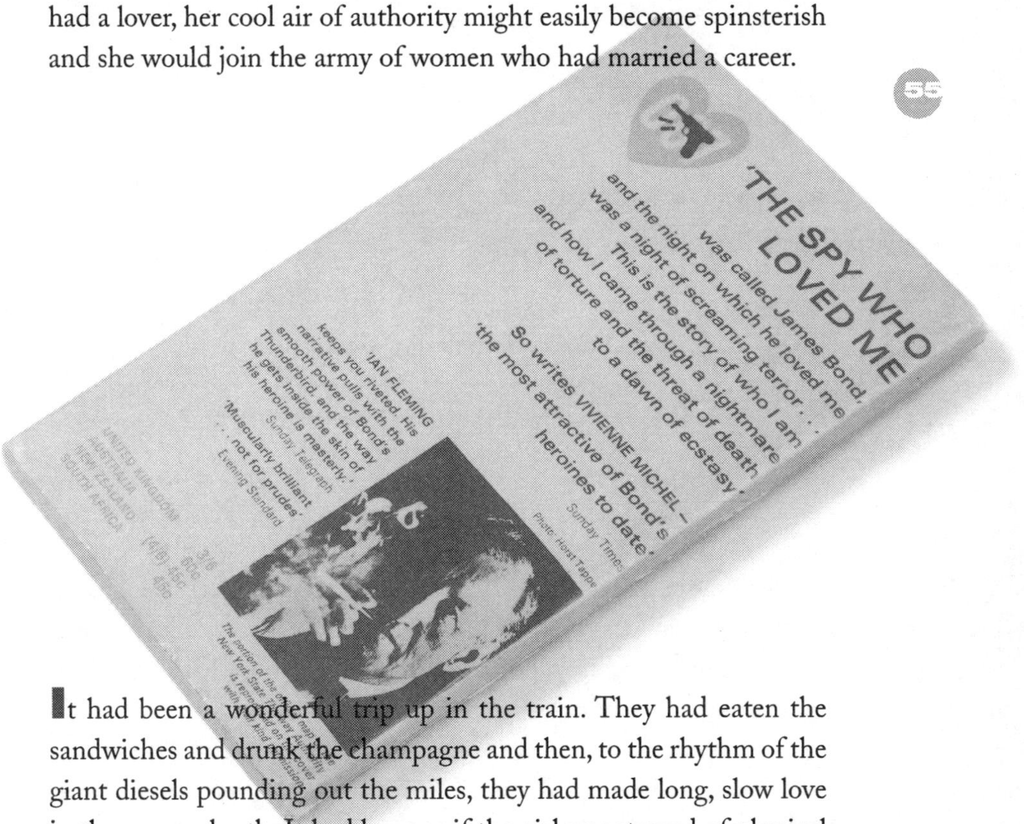

THE SPY WHO LOVED ME

... was called James Bond, and the night on which he loved me was a night of screaming terror ...

This is the story of who I am and how I came through a nightmare of torture and the threat of death to a dawn of ecstasy.

So writes VIVIENNE MICHEL – 'the most attractive of Bond's heroines to date'.

Sunday Times

'IAN FLEMING keeps you riveted ... His narrative pulls with the smooth power of Bond's Thunderbird, and the way he gets inside the skin of his heroine is masterly.'

Sunday Telegraph

'Muscularly brilliant ... not for prudes'

Evening Standard

UNITED KINGDOM
AUSTRALIA
NEW ZEALAND
SOUTH AFRICA

3/6
60c
67½c
45c

It had been a wonderful trip up in the train. They had eaten the sandwiches and drunk the champagne and then, to the rhythm of the giant diesels pounding out the miles, they had made long, slow love in the narrow berth. It had been as if the girl was starved of physical love. She had woken him twice more in the night with soft demanding caresses, saying nothing, just reaching for his hard lean body. The next day she had twice pulled down the roller blinds to shut out the hard light and had taken him by the hand and said, 'Love me, James' as if she was a child asking for a sweet.

A naked arm smelling of Chanel No. 5 snaked around his neck and warm lips kissed the corner of his mouth. As he reached up to hold the arm where it was, a breathless voice said, 'Oh James! I'm sorry. I just had to!'

Not bothering to open the low door of the MG, the girl swung one brown leg and then the other over the side of the car, showing her thighs under the pleated cream cotton skirt almost to her waist, and slipped to the pavement.

He gazed for a moment into the mirror and wondered about Vesper's morals. He wanted her cold and arrogant body. He wanted to see tears and desire in her remote blue eyes and to take the ropes of her black hair in his hands and bend her long body back under his.

She had a gay, to-hell-with-you face that, Bond thought, would become animal in passion. In bed she would fight and bite and then suddenly melt into hot surrender. He could almost see the proud, sensual mouth bare away from the even white teeth in a snarl of desire and then, afterwards, soften into a half-pout of loving slavery.

She was sitting, half-naked, astride a chair in front of the dressing-table, gazing across the back of the chair into the triple mirror. Her bare arms were folded along the tall back of the chair and her chin was resting on her arms. Her spine was arched, and there was arrogance in the set of her head and shoulders. The black string of her brassière across the naked back, the tight black lace pants and the splay of her legs whipped at Bond's senses.

The girl raised her eyes from looking at her face and inspected him in the mirror, briefly and coolly.

'I guess you're the new help,' she said in a low, rather husky voice that made no commitment.

Kissy's crawl was steady and relaxed and Bond had no difficulty in following the twinkling feet and the twin white mounds of her behind, divided excitingly by the black cord.

Gosh, what a crew! Even the Mafia had come in. How had Goldfinger persuaded them all to come? And who in heaven's name was Miss Pussy Galore?

There was a Pan-American Airways label attached to the grip. It said *Miss T. Case*. T? Bond walked back to his chair. Teresa? Tess? Thelma? Trudy? Tilly? None of them seemed to fit. Surely not Trixie, or Tony or Tommy.

She said, ‘People keep on asking if I'd like an alcohol rub and I keep on saying that if anyone's going to rub me it's you, and if I'm going to be rubbed with anything it's you I'd like to be rubbed with.’

Her skin was lightly tanned and without make-up except for a deep red on the lips, which were full and soft and rather moody so as to give the effect of what is called ‘a sinful mouth’. But not, thought Bond, one that often sinned – if one was to judge by the level eyes and the hint of authority and tension behind them.

With blue-black hair, blue eyes, and 37–22–35, [she] was a honey and there was a private five-pound sweep in the Section as to who would get her first.

He looked the ridiculously beautiful wild girl up and down. This was good hard English stock spiced with the hot peppers of a tropical childhood. Dangerous mixture.

Bond awoke lazily. The feel of the sand reminded him where he was. He glanced at his watch. Ten o'clock. The sun through the round thick leaves of the sea-grape was already hot. A larger shadow moved across the dappled sand in front of his face. Quarrel? Bond shifted his head and peered through the fringe of leaves and grass that concealed him from the beach. He stiffened. His heart missed a beat and then began pounding so that he had to breathe deeply to quieten it. His eyes, as he stared through the blades of grass, were fierce slits.

It was a naked girl, with her back to him. She was not quite naked. She wore a broad leather belt round her waist with a hunting knife in a leather sheath at her right hip. The belt made her nakedness extraordinarily erotic. She stood not more than five yards away on the tideline looking down at something in her hand. She stood in the classical relaxed pose of the nude, all the weight on the right leg and the left knee bent and turning slightly inwards, the head to one side as she examined the things in her hand.

It was a beautiful back. The skin was a very light uniform *café au lait* with the sheen of dull satin. The gentle curve of the backbone was deeply indented, suggesting more powerful muscles than is usual in a woman, and the behind was almost as firm and rounded as a boy's. The legs were straight and beautiful and no pinkness showed under the slightly lifted left heel. She was not a coloured girl.

Her hair was ash blonde. It was cut to the shoulders and hung there and along the side of her bent cheek in thick wet strands. A green mask was pushed back above her forehead, and the green rubber thong bound her hair at the back.

The whole scene, the empty beach, the green and blue sea, the naked girl with the strands of fair hair, reminded Bond of something. He searched his mind. Yes, she was Botticelli's Venus, seen from behind.

She had pale, Rupert Brooke good looks with high cheekbones and a beautiful jawline. She had the only violet eyes Bond had ever seen. They were the true deep violet of a pansy and they looked candidly out at the world from beneath straight black brows. Her hair, which was as black as Tilly Masterton’s, was worn in an untidy urchin cut. The mouth was a decisive slash of deep vermilion. Bond thought she was superb and so, he noticed, did Tilly Masterton, who was gazing at Miss Galore with worshipping eyes and lips that yearned. Bond decided that all was now clear to him about Tilly Masterton.

She could have been a model – probably had been before she became a hotel receptionist – that respectable female calling that yet has a whiff of the high *demi-monde* about it – and she still moved her beautiful body with the unselfconscious grace of someone who is used to going about with nothing, or practically nothing on.

Bond suddenly thought, Hell! I’ll never find another girl like this one. She’s got everything I’ve looked for in a woman. She’s beautiful, in bed and out. She’s adventurous, brave, resourceful. She’s exciting always. She seems to love me. She’d let me go on with my life. She’s a lone girl, not cluttered up with friends, relations, belongings.

These were men who had gone to war. Even Pussy Galore, in a black Dacron mackintosh with a black leather belt, looked like some young SS guardsman.

She put her hands behind her head to keep the sand out of her straggling hair and lay waiting, her eyes half hidden behind the dark mesh of her eyelashes.

The mounded vee of the bikini looked up at Bond and the proud breasts in the tight cups were two more eyes. Bond felt his control going.

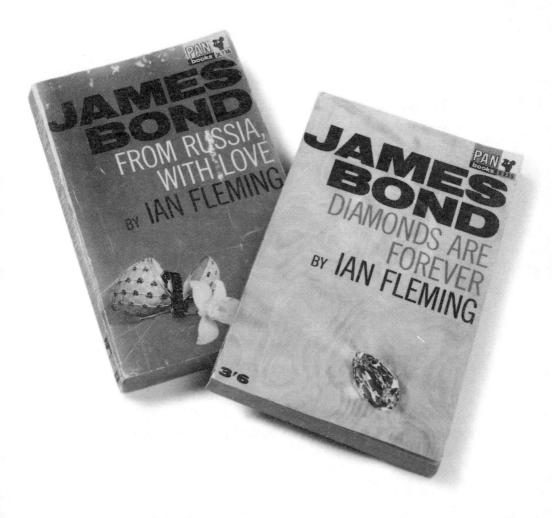

THE HOUSEKEEPER
A treasure called May

He had a small but comfortable flat off the King's Road, an elderly Scottish housekeeper – a treasure called May . . .

His mind drifted into a world of tennis courts and lily ponds and kings and queens, of London, of people being photographed with pigeons on their heads in Trafalgar Square, of the forsythia that would soon be blazing on the bypass roundabouts, of May, the treasured housekeeper in his flat off the King's Road, getting up to brew herself a cup of tea (here it was eleven o'clock. It would be four o'clock in London) . . .

May, Bond's elderly Scottish treasure, came in to clear the breakfast things away.

May, an elderly Scotswoman with iron grey hair and a handsome closed face, came in with the tray and put it on the table in the bay window with *The Times*, the only paper Bond ever read.

His treasured Scottish housekeeper . . . May, an elderly Scotswoman with iron grey hair and a handsome closed face . . .

And in the evenings there would be Tiffany in the spare room of his flat off the King's Road. He would have to send a cable to May to get things fixed. Let's see – flowers, bath essence from Floris, air the sheets . . .

May was fiddling with the breakfast things – her signal that she had something to say. Bond looked up from the centre news pages of *The Times*. 'Anything on your mind, May?'

May's elderly severe features were flushed. She said defensively, 'I have that.' She looked straight at Bond. She was holding the yoghurt carton in her hand. She crumpled it in her strong fingers and dropped it among the breakfast things on the tray. 'It's not my place to say it, Mister James, but ye're poisoning yersel'.'

Bond made his plan for the evening. He would first do an extremely careful packing job of his single suitcase, the one that had no tricks to it, have two double vodkas and tonics with a dash of Angostura, eat a large dish of May's speciality – scrambled eggs *fines herbes* – have two more vodkas and tonics, and then, slightly drunk, go to bed with half a grain of Seconal.

For the rest of the year, until May polished them up for the occasion, the medals gathered dust in some secret repository where May kept them.

'**A**nd why didn't he go and have a look at his flat? He's got some sort of a housekeeper there, Scotswoman called May, who's always sworn he was still alive and has kept the place going on her savings.'

INSIDE THE GARDEN OF DEATH

[From *You Only Live Twice*. Bond has just got inside
Dr Shatterhand's Japanese castle.]

Bond kept close to the boundary wall, flitting like a bat across the
open spaces between clumps of bushes and trees. Although his hands
were covered with the black material of the *ninja* suit, he avoided
contact with the vegetation, which emitted a continually changing
variety of strong odours and scents amongst which he recognised, as
a result of ancient adventures in the Caribbean, only the sugary perfume of dogwood. He came to the lake, a wide silent shimmer of silver from which rose the thin cloud of steam he remembered from the
aerial photograph. As he stood and watched it, a large leaf from one
of the surrounding trees came wafting down and settled on the surface near him. At once a quick, purposeful ripple swept down on the
leaf from the surrounding water and immediately subsided. There
were some kind of fish in the lake and they would be carnivores. Only
carnivores would be excited like that at the hint of a prey. Beyond the
lake, Bond came on the first of the fumaroles, a sulphurous, bubbling
pool of mud that constantly shuddered and spouted up little foun-
tains. From yards away, Bond could feel its heat. Jets of stinking
steam puffed out and disappeared, wraithlike, towards the sky. And
now the jagged silhouette of the castle, with its winged turrets,
showed above the tree-line, and Bond crept forward with added cau-
tion, alert for the moment when he would come upon the treacher-
ous gravel that surrounded it. Suddenly, through a belt of trees,

he was facing it. He stopped in the shelter of the trees, his heart hammering under his ribcage ...

Bond was now on the castle side of the lake. He heard a noise and edged behind a tree. The distant crashing in the shrubbery sounded like a wounded animal, but then, down the path, came staggering a man, or what had once been a man. The brilliant moonlight showed a head swollen to the size of a football, and only small slits remained where the eyes and mouth had been. The man moaned softly as he zigzagged along, and Bond could see that his hands were up to his puffed face and that he was trying to prise apart the swollen skin around his eyes so that he could see out. Every now and then he stopped and let out one word in an agonizing howl to the moon. It was not a howl of fear or of pain, but of dreadful supplication. Suddenly he stopped. He seemed to see the lake for the first time. With a terrible cry, and holding out his arms as if to meet a loved one, he made a quick run to the edge and threw himself in. At once there came the swirl of movement Bond had noticed before, but this time it involved a great area of water and there was a wild boiling of the surface around the vaguely threshing body. A mass of small fish were struggling to get at the man, particularly at the naked hands and face, and their six-inch bodies glittered and flashed in the moonlight. Once the man raised his head and let out a single, terrible scream and Bond saw that his face was encrusted with pendent fish as if with silvery locks of hair. Then his head fell back into the lake and he rolled over and over as if trying to rid himself of his attackers. But slowly the black stain spread and spread around him and finally, perhaps because his jugular had been pierced, he lay still, face downwards in the water, and his head jigged slightly with the ceaseless momentum of the attack.

James Bond wiped the cold sweat off his face. Piranha! The South American fresh-water killer whose massive jaws and flat, razor-sharp teeth can strip a horse down to the bones in under an hour! And this man had been one of the suicides who had heard of this terrible death! He had come searching for the lake and had got his face poisoned by some pretty shrub. The Herr Doktor had certainly provided a feast for his victims. Unending dishes for their delectation! A true banquet of death!

James Bond shuddered and went on his way. All right, Blofeld, he thought, that's one more notch on the sword that is already on its way to your neck. Brave words! Bond hugged the wall and kept going. Gunmetal was showing in the east.

But the Garden of Death hadn't quite finished the display of its wares.

All over the park, a slight smell of sulphur hung in the air, and many times Bond had had to detour around steaming cracks in the ground and the quaking mud of fumaroles, identified by a warning circle of white-painted stones. The Doctor was most careful lest anyone should fall into one of these liquid furnaces by mistake! But now Bond came to one the size of a circular tennis-court, and here there was a rough shrine in the grotto at the back of it and, dainty touch, a vase with flowers in it – chrysanthemums, because it was now officially winter and therefore the chrysanthemum season. They were arranged with some sprigs of dwarf maple, in a pattern which no doubt spelled out some fragrant message to the initiates of Japanese flower arrangement. And opposite the grotto, behind which Bond in his ghostly black uniform crouched in concealment, a Japanese gentleman stood in rapt contemplation of the bursting mud-boils that were erupting genteelly in the simmering soup of the pool. James Bond thought 'gentleman' because the man was dressed in the top hat, frock-coat, striped trousers, stiff collar and spats of a high government official – or of the father of the bride. And the gentleman held a carefully rolled umbrella between his clasped hands, and his head was bowed over its crook as if in penance. He was speaking, in a soft compulsive babble, like someone in a highly ritualistic church, but he made no gestures and just stood, humbly, quietly, either confessing or asking one of the gods for something.

Bond stood against a tree, black in the blackness. He felt he should intervene in what he knew to be the man's purpose. But how to do so knowing no Japanese, having nothing but his 'deaf and dumb' card to show? And it was vital that he should remain a 'ghost' in the garden, not get involved in some daft argument with a man he didn't know, about some ancient sin he could never understand. So Bond stood, while the trees threw long black arms across the scene, and waited with a cold, closed, stone face, for death to walk on stage.

The man stopped talking. He raised his head and gazed up at the moon. He politely lifted his shining top hat. Then he replaced it, tucked his umbrella under one arm and sharply clapped his hands. Then walking, as if to a business appointment, calmly, purposefully, he took the few steps to the edge of the bubbling fumarole, stepped carefully over the warning stones and went on walking. He sank slowly in the glutinous grey slime and not a sound escaped his lips until, as the tremendous heat reached his groin, he uttered one rasping 'Arrghh!' and the gold in his teeth showed as his head arched back in the rictus of death. Then he was gone and only the top hat remained, tossing on a small fountain of mud that spat intermittently into the air. Then the hat slowly crumpled with the heat and disappeared, and a great belch was uttered from the belly of the fumarole and a horrible stench of cooking meat overcame the pervading stink of sulphur and reached Bond's nostrils.

FOREIGN TRAVEL
This country of furtive,
stunted little men

So that was it! The old Hun again. Always at your feet or at your throat! Sense of humour indeed!

'**T**here's nothing so extraordinary about American gangsters,' protested Bond. 'They're not Americans. Mostly a lot of Italian bums with monogrammed shirts who spend the day eating spaghetti and meat-balls and squirting scent over themselves.'

He got up from the bed. At least they would soon be out of these damned Balkans and down into Italy. Then Switzerland, France – among friendly people, away from the furtive lands.

'**W**e don't see many of those [Bulgarians] around. They're mostly used against the Turks and the Yugoslavs. They're stupid, but obedient. The Russians use them for simple killings or as fall-guys for more complicated ones.'

Bond said angrily, 'Balls to you, Tiger! And balls again! Just because you're a pack of militant potential murderers here, longing to get rid of your American masters and play at being *samurai* again, snarling behind your subservient smiles, you only judge people by your own jungle standards. Let me tell you this, my fine friend. England may have been bled pretty thin by a couple of World Wars, our Welfare State politics may have made us expect too much for free, and the liberation of our Colonies may have gone too fast, but we still climb Everest and beat plenty of the world at plenty of sports and win Nobel Prizes. Our politicians may be a feather-pated bunch, and I expect yours are too. All politicians are. But there's nothing wrong with the British people – although there are only fifty million of them.'

She had the gay, bold, forthcoming looks the Viennese are supposed to have and seldom do.

Bond reflected that good Americans were fine people and that most of them seemed to come from Texas.

I used to think your gangsters were just a bunch of Italian greaseballs who filled themselves with pizza pie and beer all the week and on Saturdays knocked off a garage or drug store so as to pay their way at the races. But they've certainly got plenty of violence on the payroll.'

The best things in America are chipmunks, and oyster stew.

Bond's experience told him that few of the Asiatic races were courageous gamblers, even the much-vaunted Chinese being inclined to lose heart if the going was bad.

The fat man was grinning delightedly. He came up with Bond and, to Bond's horror, threw open his arms, clutched Bond to him and kissed him on both cheeks.

Bond said: 'For God's sake, Colombo.'

Tiger held up a hand. 'And that is another thing. No swearing, please. There are no swear-words in the Japanese languages and the usage of bad language does not exist.'

'But good heavens, Tiger! No self-respecting man could get through the day without his battery of four-letter words to cope with the roughage of life and let off steam. If you're late for a vital appointment with your superiors, and you find that you've left all your papers at home, surely you say, well Freddie Uncle Charlie Katie, if I may put it so as not to offend.'

He'd never liked being up against the Chinese. There were too many of them.

Bond reflected it was no wonder that the Big Man found Voodoo-ism such a powerful weapon on minds that still recoiled at a white chicken's feather or crossed sticks in the road – right in the middle of the shining capital city of the Western world.

'I'm glad we came up here,' said Bond. 'I'm beginning to get the hang of Mr Big. One just doesn't catch the smell of all this in a country like England. We're a superstitious lot there of course – particularly the Celts – but here one can almost hear the drums.'

Bond had never cared for Orléans. It was a priest and myth ridden town without charm or gaiety. It was content to live off Joan of Arc and give the visitor a hard, holy glare while it took his money.

What a man for Head of Station T! His size alone, in this country of furtive, stunted little men, would give him authority, and his giant vitality and love of life would make everyone his friend.

Kerim harangued the waiter. He sat back, smiling at Bond. 'That is the only way to treat these damned people [the Turks]. They love to be cursed and kicked. It is all they understand. It is in the blood. All this pretence of democracy is killing them. They want some sultans and wars and rape and fun. Poor brutes, in their striped suits and bowler hats.'

'I knew it was Uhlmann, the ex-Gestapo man. One's had to get to know the smell of a German, and of a Russian for that matter, in my line of work.'

'I don't think I've ever heard of a great negro criminal before,' said Bond. 'Chinamen, of course, the men behind the opium trade. There've been some big-time Japs, mostly in pearls and drugs. Plenty of negroes mixed up in diamonds and gold in Africa, but always in a small way. They don't seem to take to big business. Pretty law-abiding chaps I should have thought except when they've drunk too much.'

'Our man's a bit of an exception,' said M. 'He's not pure negro. Born in Haiti. Good dose of French blood. Trained in Moscow, too, as you'll see from the file. And the negro races are just beginning to throw up geniuses in all the professions – scientists, doctors, writers. It's about time they turned out a great criminal. After all, there are 250,000,000 of them in the world. Nearly a third of the white population. They've got plenty of brains and ability and guts. And now Moscow's taught one of them the technique.'

'What's he so worried about? It's not as if this was Iron Curtain business. America's a civilized country. More or less.'

Why hadn't M chosen a Jap speaker? Bond had never been east of Hong Kong. But then Orientalists had their own particular draw-backs – too much tied up with tea ceremonies and flower arrange-ments and Zen and so forth.

Wherever he had gone in America he had left dead bodies. Bond was glad to be on his way to the soft green flanks of Jamaica and to be leaving behind the great hard continent of Eldollarado.

Darko Kerim had a wonderfully warm dry handclasp. It was a strong Western handful of operative fingers – not the banana skin handshake of the East that makes you want to wipe your fingers on your coat-tails.

Tiger Tanaka's face darkened perceptibly. 'For the time being,' he said with distaste, 'we are being subjected to what I can best describe as the "Scuola di Coca-Cola". Baseball, amusement arcades, hot dogs, hideously large bosoms, neon lighting – these are part of our payment for defeat in battle.'

SEX
They were like two loving animals

Again there were the two piles of clothes on the floor, and the two whispering bodies on the banquette, and the slow searching hands. And the love-knot was formed, and, as the train jolted over the points into the echoing station of Venice, there came the final lost despairing cry.

With most women his manner was a mixture of taciturnity and passion. The lengthy approaches to a seduction bored him almost as much as the subsequent mess of disentanglement. He found something grisly in the inevitability of the pattern of each affair. The conventional parabola – sentiment, the touch of the hand, the kiss, the passionate kiss, the feel of the body, the climax in the bed, then more bed, then less bed, then the boredom, the tears and the final bitterness – was to him shameful and hypocritical. Even more he shunned the *mise en scène* for each of these acts in the play – the meeting at a party, the restaurant, the taxi, his flat, her flat, then the weekend by the sea, then the flats again, then the furtive alibis and the final angry farewell on some doorstep in the rain.

He got up and went down on one knee beside her. He picked up her hand and looked into it. At the base of the thumb the Mount of Venus swelled luxuriously. Bond bent his head down into the warm soft hand and bit softly into the swelling. He felt her other hand in his hair. He bit harder. The hand he was holding curled round his mouth. She was panting. He bit still harder. She gave a little scream and wrenched his head away by the hair.

'What are you doing?'

The half-stripped body splayed above him on the surface as he swam up from below; the soft-hard quick kiss with his arms about her; the pointed hillocks of her breasts, so close to him, and the soft flat stomach descending to the mystery of her tightly closed thighs.

To hell with it.

Bond came to the conclusion that Tilly Masterton was one of those girls whose hormones had got mixed up. He knew the type well and thought they and their male counterparts were a direct consequence of giving votes to women and 'sex equality'. As a result of fifty years of emancipation, feminine qualities were dying out or being transferred to the males. Pansies of both sexes were everywhere, not yet completely homosexual, but confused, not knowing what they were. The result was a herd of unhappy sexual misfits – barren and full of frustrations, the women wanting to dominate and the men to be nannied. He was sorry for them, but he had no time for them.

Bond took out his handkerchief and wiped his face. Where the hell was the girl? Had she been caught? Had she had second thoughts? Had he been too rough with her last night, or rather this morning, in the great bed?

While his mouth went on kissing her, his hand went to her left breast and held it, feeling the peak hard with desire under his fingers. His hand strayed on down the flat stomach. Her legs shifted languidly. She moaned softly and her mouth slid away from his. Below the closed eyes the long lashes quivered like humming birds' wings.

He felt a wave of disquiet. It had been a bad break coming across this girl. In combat, like it or not, a girl is your extra heart. The enemy has two targets against your one.

They flaunted their bodies at him, paused and chattered to see if he would respond, and, when he didn't, linked arms and sauntered on towards the town, leaving Bond wondering why it was that French girls had more prominent navels than any others.

If there was one thing that set James Bond really moving in life, with the exception of gun-play, it was being passed at speed by a pretty girl.

She paused and smiled at him. 'Now it's your turn again,' she said. 'Buy me another drink and then tell me what sort of a woman you think would add to you.'

Bond gave his order to the steward. He lit a cigarette and turned back to her. 'Somebody who can make Sauce Béarnaise as well as love,' he said.

'Holy mackerel! Just any old dumb hag who can cook and lie on her back?'

'Oh, no. She's got to have all the usual things that all women have.' Bond examined her. 'Gold hair. Grey eyes. A sinful mouth. Perfect figure. And of course she's got to make lots of funny jokes and know how to dress and play cards and so forth. The usual things.'

With him she had no inhibitions. They were like two loving animals. It was natural. She had no shame.

He felt the sexual challenge all beautiful Lesbians have for men.

Was it true what The Big Man had said, that she would have nothing to do with men? He doubted it. She seemed open to love and to desire. At any rate he knew she was not closed to him. He wanted her to come back and sit down opposite him again so that he could look at her and play with her and slowly discover her.

Had there been the prudery of a virgin? Bond thought not. There was the confidence of having been loved in the proud breasts and the insolently lilting behind – the assertion of a body that knows what it can be for.

Oh, lord! thought Bond. One of those! A girl with a wing, perhaps two wings, down.

Names like Ruby, Violet, Pearl, Anne, Elizabeth, Beryl, sounded in his ears, but all he saw was a sea of beautiful, sunburned faces and a succession of splendid, sweatered young bosoms.

Bond looked thoughtfully at the girl. He decided it would be ungallant to spank her, so to speak, on an empty stomach.

Bond saw luck as a woman, to be softly wooed or brutally ravaged, never pandered to or pursued.

Why the hell couldn't they stay at home and mind their pots and pans and stick to their frocks and gossip and leave men's work to the men.

Bond awoke in his own room at dawn and for a time he lay and stroked his memories.

Bond put an arm round her and held her to him. 'My darling.' He knew that nothing but the great step of physical love would cure these misunderstandings, but that words and time still had to be wasted.

Women are often meticulous and safe drivers, but they are very seldom first-class. In general Bond regarded them as a mild hazard and he always gave them plenty of road and was ready for the unpredictable.

Bond was not amused. 'What the hell do they want to send me a woman for?' he said bitterly. 'Do they think this is a bloody picnic?'

Mathis interrupted. 'Calm yourself, my dear James. She is as serious as you could wish and as cold as an icicle.'

As soon as Bond had hit the shot he knew it wouldn't do. The difference between a good golf shot and a bad one is the same as the difference between a beautiful and a plain woman – a matter of millimetres.

Once he had taken her by the hand it would be for ever. He would be in the role of the healer, the analyst, to whom the patient had transferred her love and trust on her way out of the illness. There would be no cruelty equal to dropping her hand once he had taken it in his. Was he ready for all that that meant in his life and his career?

Bond stirred in his bunk and put the problem away. It was too early for that.

What would she use? English girls made mistakes about scent. He hoped it would be something slight and clean. Balmain's *Vent Vert* perhaps, or Caron's *Muguet*.

'My darling,' he said. He plunged his mouth down on to hers, forcing her teeth apart with his tongue and feeling her own tongue working at first shyly then more passionately. He slipped his hands down to her swelling buttocks and gripped them fiercely, pressing the centres of their bodies together.

His growing warmth towards Solitaire and his desire for her body were in a compartment which had no communicating door with his professional life.

Vesper looked at him thoughtfully.

'People are islands,' she said. 'They don't really touch. However close they are, they're really quite separate. Even if they've been married for fifty years.'

Bond thought with dismay that she must be going into a *vin triste*. Too much champagne had made her melancholy.

82

'**A**re you married?' She paused. 'Or anything?'

'No. I occasionally have affairs.'

'So you're one of those old-fashioned men who like sleeping with women. Why haven't you ever married?'

'I expect because I think I can handle life better on my own. Most marriages don't add two people together. They subtract one from the other.'

Tiffany thought this over.

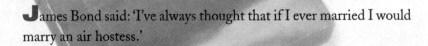

James Bond said: 'I've always thought that if I ever married I would marry an air hostess.'

CARS

His tyres screamed
on the tarmac

Bond's car was his only personal hobby. One of the last of the 4½ -litre Bentleys with the supercharger by Amherst Villiers, he had bought it almost new in 1933 and had kept it in careful storage through the war. It was still serviced every year and, in London, a former Bentley mechanic, who worked in a garage near Bond's Chelsea flat, tended it with jealous care. Bond drove it hard and well and with an almost sensual pleasure. It was a battleship-grey convertible coupe, which really did convert, and it was capable of touring at ninety with thirty miles an hour in reserve.

He motored slowly over to Reculver, savouring the evening and the drink inside him and the quiet bubble of the twin exhausts.

'Well, I'll be damned,' said Bond incredulously. 'But what sort of a car is this anyway? Isn't it a Studebaker?'

'Studillac,' said Leiter. 'Studebaker with a Cadillac engine. Special transmission and brakes and rear axle. A small firm near New York turns them out. Only a few, but they're a damned sight better sports car than those Corvettes and Thunderbirds.'

Bond had the most selfish car in England. It was a Mark II Continental Bentley that some rich idiot had married to a telegraph pole on the Great West Road. Bond had bought the bits for £1,500 and Rolls had straightened the bend in the chassis and fitted new clockwork – the Mark IV engine with 9.5 compression. Then Bond had gone to Mulliners with £3,000, which was half his total capital, and they had sawn off the old cramped sports saloon body and had fitted a trim, rather square convertible two-seater affair, power-operated, with only two large armed bucket-seats in black leather. The rest of the blunt end was all knife-edged, rather ugly, boot. The car was painted in rough, not gloss, battleship grey and the upholstery was black morocco. She went like a bird and a bomb and Bond loved her more than all the women at present in his life rolled, if that were feasible, together . . .

The twin exhausts – Bond had demanded two-inch pipes; he hadn't liked the old soft flutter of the marque – growled solidly as the long grey nose topped by a big octagonal silver bolt instead of the winged B, swerved out of the little Chelsea square and into King's Road.

Almost exactly twenty-four hours before, James Bond had been nursing his car, the old continental Bentley – the 'R' type chassis with the big 6 engine and a 13:40 back-axle ratio – that he had now been driving for three years, along that fast but dull stretch of N1 between Abbeville and Montreuil.

He leaned forward and flicked down the red switch. The moan of the blower died away and there was silence in the car as he motored along, easing his tense muscles. He wondered if the supercharger had damaged the engine. Against the solemn warnings of Rolls-Royce, he had had fitted, by his pet expert at the Headquarters' motor pool, an Arnott supercharger controlled by a magnetic clutch. Rolls-Royce had said the crankshaft bearings wouldn't take the extra load and, when he confessed to them what he had done, they regretfully but firmly withdrew their guarantees and washed their hands of their bastardized child. This was the first time he had notched 125 and the rev counter had hovered dangerously over the red area at 4500. But the temperature and oil were OK and there were no expensive noises. And, by God, it had been fun!

James Bond flung the DB III through the last mile of straight and did a racing change down into third and then into second for the short hill before the inevitable traffic crawl through Rochester. Leashed in by the velvet claw of the front discs, the engine muttered its protest with a mild back-popple from the twin exhausts.

... the DB III had ... certain extras which might or might not come in handy. These included switches to alter the type and colour of Bond's front and rear lights if he was following or being followed at night, reinforced steel bumpers, fore and aft, in case he needed to ram, a long-barrelled Colt .45 in a trick compartment under the driver's seat, a radio pick-up tuned to receive an apparatus called the Homer, and plenty of concealed space that would fox most Customs men.

Bond liked fast cars and he liked driving them. Most American cars bored him. They lacked personality and the patina of individual craftsmanship that European cars have. They were just 'vehicles', similar in shape and in colour, and even in the tone of their horns. Designed to serve for a year and then be turned in in part exchange for the next year's model. All the fun of driving had been taken out of them with the abolition of a gear-change, with hydraulic-assisted steering and spongy suspension. All effort had been smoothed away and all of that close contact with the machine and the road that extracts skill and nerve from the European driver. To Bond, American cars were just beetle-shaped Dodgems in which you motored along with one hand on the wheel, the radio full on, and the power-operated windows closed to keep out the draughts.

But Leiter had got hold of an old Cord, one of the few American cars with a personality, and it cheered Bond to climb into the low-hung saloon, to hear the solid bite of the gears and the masculine tone of the wide exhaust. Fifteen years old, he reflected, yet still one of the most modern-looking cars in the world.

Bond did a racing change and swung the big car left at the Charing fork, preferring the clear road by Chilham and Canterbury to the bottlenecks of Ashford and Folkestone. The car howled up to eighty in third and he held it in the same gear to negotiate the hairpin at the top of the long gradient leading up to the Molash road.

Bond raced back to his car, whipped into third, and went after him.

Thank God the Mercedes was white. There it went, its stop-lights blazing briefly at the intersections, the headlamps full on and the horn blaring at any hint of a check in the sparse traffic.

Bond set his teeth and rode his car as if she was a Lipizaner at the Spanish Riding School in Vienna. He could not use headlights or horn for fear of betraying his presence to the car in front. He just had to play on his brakes and gears and hope for the best.

The deep note of his two-inch exhaust thundered back at him from the houses on either side and his tyres screamed on the tarmac. He thanked heavens for the new set of racing Michelins that were only a week old.

TATIANA AND ROSA KLEBB

[From *From Russia with Love*. Tatiana is being briefed by Klebb in the privacy of Klebb's apartment on her mission to seduce Bond.]

'You will be equipped with beautiful clothes [said Klebb]. You will be instructed in all the arts of allurement. Then you will be sent to a foreign country, somewhere in Europe. There you will meet this man. You will seduce him. In this matter you will have no silly compunctions. Your body belongs to the State. Since your birth, the State has nourished it. Now your body must work for the State. Is that understood?'

'Yes, Comrade Colonel.' The logic was inescapable.

'You will accompany this man to England. There, you will no doubt be questioned. The questioning will be easy. The English do not use harsh methods. You will give such answers as you can without endangering the State. We will supply you with certain answers which we would like to be given. You will probably be sent to Canada. That is where the English send a certain category of foreign prisoner. You will be rescued and brought back to Moscow.' Rosa Klebb peered at the girl. She seemed to be accepting all this without question. 'You see, it is a comparatively simple matter. Have you any questions at this stage?'

'What will happen to the man, Comrade Colonel?'

'That is a matter of indifference to us. We shall simply use him as a means to introduce you into England. The object of the operation is to give false information to the British. We shall, of course,

Comrade, be very glad to have your own impressions of life in England. The reports of a highly trained and intelligent girl such as yourself will be of great value to the State.'

'Really, Comrade Colonel!' Tatiana felt important. Suddenly it all sounded exciting. If only she could do it well. She would assuredly do her very best. But supposing she could not make the English spy love her. She looked again at the photograph. She put her head on one side. It was an attractive face. What were these 'arts of allurement' that the woman had talked about? What could they be? Perhaps they would help.

Satisfied, Rosa Klebb got up from the table. 'And now we can relax, my dear. Work is over for the night. I will go and tidy up and we will have a friendly chat together. I shan't be a moment. Eat up those chocolates or they will go to waste.' Rosa Klebb made a vague gesture of the hand and disappeared with a preoccupied look into the next room.

Tatiana sat back in her chair. So that was what it was all about! It really wasn't so bad after all. What a relief! And what an honour to have been chosen. How silly to have been so frightened! Naturally the great leaders of the State would not allow harm to come to an innocent citizen who worked hard and had no black marks on her zapiska. Suddenly she felt immensely grateful to the father-figure that was the State, and proud that she would now have a chance to repay some of her debt. Even the Klebb woman wasn't really so bad after all.

Tatiana was still cheerfully reviewing the situation when the bedroom door opened and 'the Klebb woman' appeared in the opening. 'What do you think of this, my dear?' Colonel Klebb opened her dumpy arms and twirled on her toes like a mannequin. She struck a pose with one arm outstretched and the other arm crooked at her waist.

Tatiana's mouth had fallen open. She shut it quickly. She searched for something to say.

Colonel Klebb of SMERSH was wearing a semi-transparent nightgown in orange *crêpe de chine*. It had scallops of the same material round the low square neckline and scallops at the wrists of the broadly flounced sleeves. Underneath could be seen a brassière consisting of two large pink satin roses. Below, she wore old-fashioned knickers of pink satin with elastic above the knees. One dimpled knee, like a yellowish coconut, appeared thrust forward between the half open folds of the nightgown in the classic stance of the modeller. The feet were enclosed in pink satin slippers with the pompoms of ostrich feathers. Rosa Klebb had taken off her spectacles and her naked face was now thick with mascara and rouge and lipstick.

She looked like the oldest and ugliest whore in the world.

Tatiana stammered, 'It's very pretty.'

'Isn't it,' twittered the woman. She went over to a broad couch in the corner of the room. It was covered with a garish piece of peasant tapestry. At the back, against the wall, were rather grimy satin cushions in pastel colours.

With a squeak of pleasure, Rosa Klebb threw herself down in the caricature of a Recamier pose. She reached up an arm and turned on a pink shaded table-lamp whose stem was a naked woman in sham Lalique glass. She patted the couch beside her.

'Turn out the top light, my dear. The switch is by the door. Then come and sit beside me. We must get to know each other better.'

Tatiana walked to the door. She switched off the top light. Her hand dropped decisively to the door knob. She turned it and opened the door and stepped coolly out into the corridor. Suddenly her nerve broke. She banged the door shut behind her and ran wildly off down the corridor with her hand over her ears against the pursuing scream that never came.

DRINKING

Champagne and benzedrine!
Never again

Bond insisted on ordering Leiter's Haig-and-Haig 'on the rocks' and then he looked carefully at the barman.

'A dry Martini,' he said. 'One. In a deep champagne goblet.'

'*Oui, monsieur.*'

'Just a moment. Three measures of Gordon's, one of vodka, half a measure of Kina Lillet. Shake it very well until it's ice-cold, then add a large thin slice of lemon-peel. Got it?'

'Certainly, monsieur.' The barman seemed pleased with the idea.

'Gosh, that's certainly a drink,' said Leiter.

'**I** hope I've made it right,' she said. 'Six to one sounds terribly strong. I've never had Vodka Martinis before.'

James Bond, with two double Bourbons inside him, sat in the final departure lounge of Miami Airport and thought about life and death.

[They] spent an hour drinking the drink that Leiter had told him was fashionable in racing circles – Bourbon and branch-water. Bond guessed that in fact the water was from the tap behind the bar, but Leiter had said that real Bourbon drinkers insist on having their whisky in the traditional style, with water from high up in the branch of the local river where it will be purest. The barman didn't seem surprised when he asked for it, and Bond was amused at the conceit.

Bond had forgotten his drink. He picked it up and, tilting his head back, swallowed the Bourbon to the last drop. The ice tinkled cheerfully against his teeth.

With his finger on the page, Bond turned to the *sommelier*: 'The Taittinger '45?'

'A fine wine, monsieur,' said the *sommelier*. 'But if Monsieur will permit,' he pointed with his pencil, 'the Blanc de Blancs Brut 1943 of the same marque is without equal.'

Bond smiled. 'So be it,' he said.

'I don't drink tea. I hate it. It's mud. Moreover it's one of the main reasons for the downfall of the British Empire.'

'**A**sk Grimley to come over, would you?'

'He's here now, sir,' said the steward, making way for the wine-waiter.

'Ah, Grimley, some vodka, please.' He turned to Bond. 'Not the stuff you had in your cocktail. This is real pre-war Wolfschmidt from Riga. Like some with your smoked salmon?'

'Very much,' said Bond.

'Then what?' asked M. 'Champagne? Personally I'm going to have a half-bottle of claret. The Mouton Rothschild '34, please, Grimley. But don't pay any attention to me, James. I'm an old man. Champagne's no good for me. We've got some good champagnes, haven't we, Grimley? None of that stuff you're always telling me about, I'm afraid, James. Don't often see it in England. Taittinger, wasn't it?'

Bond smiled at M's memory. 'Yes,' he said, 'but it's only a fad of mine. As a matter of fact, for various reasons I believe I would like to drink champagne this evening. Perhaps I could leave it to Grimley.'

The wine-waiter was pleased. 'If I may suggest it, sir, the Dom Perignon '46. I understand that France only sells it for dollars, sir, so you don't often see it in London. I believe it was a gift from the Regency Club in New York, sir. I have some on ice at the moment. It's the Chairman's favourite and he told me to have it ready every evening in case he needs it.'

Bond smiled his agreement.

'So be it, Grimley,' said M.

The waiter brought the Martinis, shaken and not stirred, as Bond had stipulated, and some slivers of lemon peel in a wine glass. Bond twisted two of them and let them sink to the bottom of his drink. He picked up his glass and looked at the girl over the rim. 'We haven't drunk to the success of a mission,' he said.

Tiffany ordered a Stinger made with white *crème de menthe* and Bond ordered the same.

Bond laughed. 'All right, Tiger. But first, more *sake*! And not in these ridiculous thimbles. I've drunk five flasks of the stuff and its effect is about the same as one double Martini. I shall need another double Martini if I am to go on demonstrating the superiority of Western instinct over the wiles of the Orient.'

'Then the usual round – hat-check girl, taxi-dancer, studio extra, waitress – until she was about twenty. Then maybe life didn't seem so good and she took to liquor. Settled in a rooming house down on one of the Florida Keys and started drinking herself to death. Got so she was known as The Boiled Sweet down there.'

He ordered dry Martinis and when the two little 'personalized' bottles appeared with the glasses and the ice they seemed so inadequate that he at once ordered four more.

When M poured him three fingers from the frosted carafe Bond took a pinch of black pepper and dropped it on the surface of the vodka. The pepper slowly settled to the bottom of the glass leaving a few grains on the surface which Bond dabbed up with the tip of a finger. Then he tossed the cold liquor well to the back of his throat and put his glass, with the dregs of the pepper at the bottom, back on the table.

M gave him a glance of rather ironical inquiry.

'It's a trick the Russians taught me that time you attached me to the Embassy in Moscow,' apologized Bond. 'There's often quite a lot of fusel oil on the surface of this stuff – at least there used to be when it was badly distilled. Poisonous. In Russia, where you get a lot of bath-tub liquor, it's an understood thing to sprinkle a little pepper in your glass. It takes the fusel oil to the bottom. I got to like the taste and now it's a habit. But I shouldn't have insulted the club Wolfschmidt,' he added with a grin.

There was a medium dry Martini with a piece of lemon peel waiting for him. Bond smiled at Leiter's memory and tasted it. It was excellent, but he didn't recognize the Vermouth.

'Made with Cresta Blanca,' explained Leiter. 'New domestic brand from California. Like it?'

'Best Vermouth I have ever tasted.'

James Bond had his first drink of the evening at Fouquet's. It was not a solid drink. One cannot drink seriously in French cafés. Out of doors on a pavement in the sun is no place for vodka or whisky or gin. A *fine à l'eau* is fairly serious, but it intoxicates without tasting very good. A *quart de champagne* or a *champagne à l'orange* is all right before luncheon, but in the evening one *quart* leads to another *quart* and a bottle of indifferent champagne is a bad foundation for the night. Pernod is possible, but it should be drunk in company, and anyway Bond had never liked the stuff because its liquorice taste reminded him of his childhood. No, in cafés you have to drink the least offensive of the musical comedy drinks that go with them, and Bond always had the same thing – an Americano – Bitter Campari, Cinzano, a large slice of lemon peel and soda. For the soda he always stipulated Perrier, for in his opinion expensive soda water was the cheapest way to improve a poor drink.

Bond sat back. The wine-waiter brought the champagne and Bond tasted it. It was ice cold and seemed to have a faint taste of strawberries. It was delicious.

On a small table beside him half a bottle of Clicquot and a glass had materialized. Without asking who the benefactor was, Bond filled the glass to the brim and drank it down in two long draughts.

The one drink too many signals itself unmistakably. His final whisky and soda in the luxurious flat in Park Lane had been no different from the ten preceding ones, but it had gone down reluctantly and had left a bitter taste and an ugly sensation of surfeit.

97

Heavy drinkers veer towards an exaggeration of their basic temperaments, the classic four – Sanguine, Phlegmatic, Choleric and Melancholic. The Sanguine drunk goes gay to the point of hysteria and idiocy. The Phlegmatic sinks into a morass of sullen gloom. The Choleric is the fighting drunk of the cartoonists who spends much of his life in prison for smashing people and things, and the Melancholic succumbs to self-pity, mawkishness and tears.

Bond said, 'And I would like a medium Vodka dry Martini – with a slice of lemon peel. Shaken and not stirred, please. I would prefer Russian or Polish vodka.'

As he bit off the miles to London Airport, pushing the big car hard so as to have plenty of time for a drink, three drinks, before the take-off, only part of his mind was on the road.

Greatly encouraged, and further stimulated by half a bottle of Mouton Rothschild '53 and a glass of ten-year-old Calvados with his three cups of coffee, he went cheerfully up the thronged steps of the Casino with the absolute certitude that this was going to be a night to remember.

He was feeling dreadful. As well as acidity and liver as a result of drinking nearly two whole bottles of champagne, he had a touch of the melancholy and spiritual deflation that were partly the after-effects of the benzedrine and partly reaction to the drama of the night before.

He sat down and ordered a double medium dry Vodka Martini, on the rocks, with lemon peel, and edged his feet up against Ruby's.

Bond cursed himself for an impulse that earlier in the day would have seemed unthinkable. Champagne and benzedrine! Never again.

M looked sharply at him. 'You look pretty dreadful, 007,' he said. 'Sit down.'

Bond was aching for a drink. He got a small glass of very old Marsala and most of a bottle of very bad Algerian wine.

Bond ordered a double gin and tonic and one whole green lime. When the drink came he cut the lime in half, dropped the two squeezed halves into the long glass, almost filled the glass with ice cubes and then poured in the tonic. He took the drink out on to the balcony, and sat and looked out across the spectacular view . . . He sat for a while, luxuriously, letting the gin relax him. He ordered another and drank it down.

Bond ordered his gin and tonic with a lime, and Quarrel a Red Stripe beer. They scanned the menu and both decided on broiled lobster followed by a rare steak with native vegetables.

The drinks came. The glasses were dripping with condensation.

[**B**ond] then ordered from Room Service a bottle of the Taittinger Blanc de Blancs that he had made his traditional drink at Royale. When the bottle, in its frosted silver bucket, came, he drank a quarter of it rather fast and then went into the bathroom and had an ice-cold shower and washed his hair with Pinaud Elixir, that prince among shampoos . . .

Leiter ordered medium dry Martinis with a slice of lemon peel. He stipulated House of Lords gin and Martini Rossi. The American gin, a much higher proof than English gin, tasted harsh to Bond. He reflected that he would have to be careful what he drank that evening . . .

Leiter extracted the lemon peel from his Martini and chewed it reflectively. The bar was filling up. It was warm and companionable – a far cry, Leiter reflected, from the inimical, electric climate of the negro pleasure-spots they would be drinking in later.

‘Bring me a whisky and soda,’ said M. ‘Sure you won't have anything?’

Bond looked at his watch. It was half-past six. ‘Could I have a dry Martini?’ he said. ‘Made with Vodka. Large slice of lemon peel.’

‘Rot-gut,’ commented M briefly as the waiter went away.

Bond put ice into his drink, filled it to the top with soda and took a long pull at it. He sat back and lit a Laurens jaune. Of course the evening would be a disaster.

When the aircraft flattened out at 30,000 feet, [Bond] ordered the first of the chain of brandies and ginger ales that was to sustain him over the Channel, a leg of the North Sea, the Kattegat, the Arctic Ocean, the Beaufort Sea, the Bering Sea and the North Pacific Ocean . . .

SMOKING
God, for a cigarette!

Bond took out his black gunmetal cigarette-box and his black-oxidized Ronson lighter and put them on the desk beside him. He lit a cigarette, one of the Macedonian blend with the three gold rings round the butt that Morlands of Grosvenor Street made for him.

'**D**o you smoke? These are Shinsei. It is an acceptable brand.'
James Bond was running out of his Morland specials. He would soon have to start on the local stuff . . . He took a cigarette and lit it. It burned rapidly with something of the effect of a slow-burning firework. It had a vague taste of American blends, but it was good and sharp on the palate and lungs like 90° proof spirits. He let the smoke out in a quiet hiss and smiled.

He was pleased to see his hands were dead steady as he took out his lighter and lit one of the Morland cigarettes with the three gold rings.

He hoped he would not disgrace himself when it came to his turn to dive. *Sake* and cigarettes! Not a good mixture to train on!

Bond softly unzipped his container and took a bite at one of his three slabs of pemmican and a short draught from his water-bottle. God, for a cigarette!

'I don't myself drink or smoke, Mr Bond. Smoking, I find the most ridiculous of all the varieties of human behaviour and practically the only one that is entirely against nature. Can you imagine a cow or any animal taking a mouthful of smouldering straw then breathing in the smoke and blowing it out through its nostrils? Pah!'

He lit a cigarette. Nowadays he was trying to keep to twenty and failing by about five.

Bond lit his first cigarette of the day – the first Royal Blend he had smoked for five years – and let the smoke come out between his teeth in a luxurious hiss.

Bond had lit up a Duke of Durham, king-size, with filter. The authoritative Consumers Union of America rates this cigarette the one with the smallest tar and nicotine content. Bond had transferred to the brand from the fragrant but powerful Morland Balkan mixture with three gold rings round the paper he had been smoking since his teens. The Dukes tasted of almost nothing, but they were at least better than Vanguards, the new 'tobaccoless' cigarette from America, that despite its health-protecting qualities, filled the room with a faint 'burning leaves' smell that made visitors to his office inquire whether 'something was on fire somewhere'.

She stopped abruptly. She said, 'Give me some more champagne. All this silly talking has made me thirsty. And I would like a packet of Players' – she laughed – 'Please, as they say in the advertisements. I am fed up with just smoking smoke. I need my Hero.'

Bond bought a packet from the cigarette girl. He said, 'What's that about a hero?'

She had entirely changed. Her bitterness had gone, and the lines of strain from her face. She had softened. She was suddenly a girl out for the evening. 'Ah, you don't know! My one true love! The man of my dreams. The sailor on the front of the packet of Players.'

Then he lit his seventieth cigarette of the day . . .

The strong, rather good hands lay quietly on his crossed arms on the counter, and now he reached down to his hip pocket and took out a wide, thin gunmetal cigarette case and opened it.

'Have one? Senior Service.'

When he coughed – smoking too much goes with drinking too much and doubles the hangover – a cloud of small luminous black spots swam across his vision like amoebae in pond water.

'It would be a start if the warmongers could be eliminated, sir.' This is for number one on the list.' The hand, snub-nosed with black metal, flashed out of the pocket...

From its breathtaking opening in London, when a brainwashed James Bond confronts his chief, 'M', to its bloody climax in the mangrove swamps of Jamaica, this is a thriller in the full tradition of its multi-million-selling predecessors.

splendidly forceful
BOOKS AND BOOKMEN

a winner
YORKSHIRE EVENING POST

Ian Fleming: photo by Horst Tappe

EATING

Breakfast was Bond's favourite meal of the day

Bond liked to make a good breakfast. After a cold shower, he sat at the writing-table in front of the window. He looked out at the beautiful day and consumed half a pint of iced orange juice, three scrambled eggs and bacon and a double portion of coffee without sugar.

Some *tagliatelle verdi* came, and the wine, and then a delicious escalope. 'Oh it is so good,' she said. 'Since I came out of Russia I am all stomach.' Her eyes widened. 'You won't let me get too fat, James. You won't let me get so fat that I am no use for making love?'

Lacquer boxes of rice, raw quails' eggs in sauce and bowls of sliced seaweed were placed in front of them both. Then they were each given a fine oval dish bearing a large lobster whose head and tail had been left as a dainty ornament to the sliced pink flesh in the centre. Bond set to with his chopsticks. He was surprised to find that the flesh was raw. He was even more surprised when the head of his lobster began moving off his dish and, with questioning antennae and scrabbling feet, tottered off across the table. 'Good God, Tiger!' Bond said, aghast. 'The damn thing's alive.'

Bond shook himself, then he picked up his knife and selected the thickest of the pieces of hot toast.

'The trouble always is,' he explained to Vesper, 'not how to get enough caviar, but how to get enough toast with it.'

They drank the cold hard drink appreciatively. Leiter with a faintly quizzical expression on his hawk-like face.

There was a knock at the door. Leiter opened it to let in the bell-boy with Bond's suitcases. He was followed by two waiters pushing trolleys with covered dishes, cutlery and snow-white linen, which they proceeded to lay out on a folding table.

'Soft-shell crabs with tartare sauce, flat beef Hamburgers, medium-rare, from the charcoal grill, french-fried potatoes, broccoli, mixed salad with thousand-island dressing, ice-cream with melted butterscotch and as good a Liebfraumilch as you can get in America. Okay?'

'It sounds fine,' said Bond with a mental reservation about the melted butterscotch.

In the restaurant car, Bond ordered Americanos and a bottle of Chianti Broglio. The wonderful European hors-d'œuvres came.

James Bond scraped the last dregs of yoghurt out of the bottom of the carton that said '*Goat-milk culture. From our own Goat Farm at Stanway, Glos. The Heart of the Cotswolds. According to an authentic Bulgarian recipe*'. He took an Energen roll, sliced it carefully – they are apt to crumble – and reached for the black treacle.

James Bond was not a gourmet. In England he lived on grilled soles, *œufs cocotte* and cold roast beef with potato salad. But when travelling abroad, generally by himself, meals were a welcome break in the day, something to break the tension of fast driving . . .

He finally chose one of his favourite restaurants in France, a modest establishment, unpromisingly placed exactly opposite the railway station of Etaples, rang up his old friend Monsieur Becaud for a table and, two hours later, was motoring back to the Casino with Turbot poche, sauce mousseline, and half the best roast partridge he had eaten in his life, under his belt.

Later, as Bond was finishing his first straight whisky 'on the rocks' and was contemplating the *pâté de foie gras* and cold *langouste* which the waiter had just laid out for him, the telephone rang.

'Yes, come on in, Quarrel. We've got a busy day. Had some break-fast?'

'Yes, tank you, cap'n. Salt fish an' ackee an' a tot of rum.'

'Good God,' said Bond. 'That's tough stuff to start the day on.'

'Mos' refreshin',' said Quarrel stolidly.

The second course came, and with it a bottle of Kavaklidere, a rich coarse burgundy like any other Balkan wine. The Kebab was good and tasted of smoked bacon fat and onions. Kerim ate a kind of Steak Tartare – a large flat hamburger of finely minced raw meat laced with peppers and chives and bound together with yolk of egg. He made Bond try a forkful. It was delicious. Bond said so.

It had everything. Propped among the bottles were two menus, huge double-folio pages covered with print. They might have been from the Savoy Grill, or the '21', or the Tour d'Argent. Bond ran his eye down one of them. It began with *Caviar double de Beluga* and ended with *Sorbet à la Champagne*. In between was every dish whose con-stituents would not be ruined by a deep freeze. Bond tossed it down. One certainly couldn't grumble about the quality of the cheese in the trap!

The waiter came and there was a brisk rattle of Italian. Bond ordered. Tagliatelle Verdi with a Genoese sauce which Kristatos said was improbably concocted of basil, garlic and pine cones.

Bond frowned. 'It's not difficult to get a Double o number if you're prepared to kill people … It's a confusing business but if it's one's profession, one does what one's told. How do you like the grated egg with your caviar?'

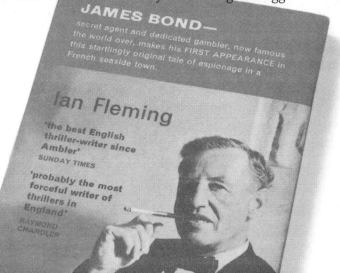

JAMES BOND—

secret agent and dedicated gambler, now famous the world over, makes his FIRST APPEARANCE in this startlingly original tale of espionage in a French seaside town.

Ian Fleming

'the best English thriller-writer since Ambler'
SUNDAY TIMES

'probably the most forceful writer of thrillers in England'
RAYMOND CHANDLER

Photo : Cecil Beaton

'**R**oom Service? I'd like to order breakfast. Half a pint of orange juice, three eggs, lightly scrambled, with bacon, a double portion of Café Espresso with cream. Toast. Marmalade. Got it?'

He thought of the bitter weather in the London streets, the grudging warmth of the hissing gas-fire in his office at Headquarters, the chalked-up menu on the pub he had passed on his last day in London: 'Giant Toad and 2 Veg.'

He stretched luxuriously.

Ma Frazier's was a cheerful contrast to the bitter streets. They had an excellent meal of Little Neck Clams and Fried Chicken Maryland with bacon and sweet corn.

'We've got to have it,' said Leiter. 'It's the national dish.'

Sam,' he called a waiter over. 'Look after these gemmums order.' He moved away.

They ordered Scotch-and-soda and chicken sandwiches.

Bond sniffed. 'Marihuana,' he commented.

'Most of the real hep-cats smoke reefers,' explained Leiter. 'Wouldn't be allowed most places.'

Room Service, good morning,' said the golden voice.

'Breakfast, please,' said Bond. 'Pineapple juice, double. Cornflakes and cream. Shirred eggs with bacon. Double portion of Café Espresso. Toast and marmalade.'

'Yes, sir,' said the girl.

Bond would have liked to stay outside the town and sleep on the banks of the Loire in the excellent Auberge de la Montespan, his belly full of *quenelles de brochet*.

'Stone crabs. Not frozen. Fresh. Melted butter. Thick toast. Right?'

'Very good, Mr Du Pont.' The wine-waiter, washing his hands, took the waiter's place.

'Two pints of pink champagne. The Pommery '50. Silver tankards. Right?'

'Vairry good, Mr Du Pont. A cocktail to start?'

Mr Du Pont turned to Bond. He smiled and raised his eyebrows.

Bond said, 'Vodka Martini, please. With a slice of lemon peel.'

. . . The Martinis came. Mr Du Pont said to the wine waiter, 'Bring two more in ten minutes.'

. . . With ceremony, a wide silver dish of crabs, big ones, their shells and claws broken, was placed in the middle of the table. A silver sauceboat brimming with melted butter and a long rack of toast was put beside each of their plates. The tankards of champagne frothed pink.

. . . The meat of the stone crabs was the tenderest, sweetest shell-fish he had ever tasted. It was perfectly set off by the dry toast and slightly burned taste of the melted butter. The champagne seemed to have the faintest scent of strawberries. It was ice cold. After each helping of crab, the champagne cleaned the palate for the next. They ate steadily and with absorption and hardly exchanged a word until the dish was cleared.

With a slight belch, Mr Du Pont for the last time wiped the butter off his chin with his silken bib and sat back.

Bond . . . walked into the station restaurant and ate one of his favourite meals – two *œufs cocotte à la crème*, a large *sole meunière* (Orléans was close enough to the sea. The fish of the Loire are inclined to be muddy) and an adequate Camembert.

The eggs came and were good. The mousseline sauce might have been mixed at Maxim's.

He looked up at the steward. 'Any of that Beluga caviar left, Porterfield?'

'Yes, sir. There was a new delivery last week.'

'Well,' said M. 'Caviar for me. Devilled kidney and a slice of your excellent bacon. Peas and new potatoes. Strawberries in kirsch. What about you, James?'

'I've got a mania for really good smoked salmon,' said Bond. Then he pointed down the menu. 'Lamb cutlets. The same vegetables as you, as it's May. Asparagus with Béarnaise sauce sounds wonderful. And perhaps a slice of pineapple.' He sat back and pushed the menu away.

'Thank heaven for a man who makes up his mind,' said M. He looked up at the steward. 'Have you got all that, Porterfield?'

'Yes, sir.' The steward smiled. 'You wouldn't care for a marrow bone after the strawberries, sir? We got half a dozen in today from the country, and I'd specially kept one in case you came in.'

'Of course. You know I can't resist them. Bad for me but it can't be helped.'

James Bond wrestled with his chopsticks and slivers of raw octopus and a mound of rice.

He turned on a cold bath and shaved patiently with cold water and hoped that the exotic breakfast he had ordered would not be a fiasco.

He was not disappointed. The yoghurt, in a blue china bowl, was deep yellow and with the consistency of thick cream. The green figs, ready peeled, were bursting with ripeness, and the Turkish coffee was jet black and with the burned taste that showed it had been freshly ground.

Breakfast was Bond's favourite meal of the day. When he was stationed in London it was always the same. It consisted of very strong coffee, from De Bry in New Oxford Street, brewed in an American Chemex, of which he drank two large cups, black and without sugar. The single egg, in the dark blue egg cup with a gold ring round the top, was boiled for three and a third minutes.

It was a fresh, speckled brown egg from French Maran hens owned by some friends of May in the country . . . Then there were two thick slices of wholewheat toast, a large pat of deep yellow Jersey butter and three squat glass jars containing Tiptree 'Little Scarlet' strawberry jam, Cooper's Vintage Oxford marmalade and Norwegian Heather Honey from Fortnum's. The coffee pot and the silver on the tray were Queen Anne, and the china was Minton, of the same dark blue and gold and white as the egg-cup.

Bond helped himself to another slice of smoked salmon from the silver dish beside him. It had the delicate glutinous texture only achieved by Highland curers – very different from the desiccated products of Scandinavia. He rolled a wafer-thin slice of brown bread-and-butter into a cylinder and contemplated it thoughtfully.

'**Y**ou like beef?'

'No,' said Bond stolidly. 'As a matter of fact, I don't . . .'

The steak came. It was accompanied by various succulent side-dishes, including a saucer of blood, which Bond refused. But the meat could be cut with a fork, and was indeed without equal in Bond's experience.

The smoked salmon was from Nova Scotia and a poor substitute for the product of Scotland, but the Brizzola was all that Leiter had said, so tender that Bond could cut it with a fork. He finished his lunch with half an avocado with French dressing and then dawdled over his Espresso.

'**L**isten, Bond,' said Tiffany Case. 'It'd take more than Crabmeat Ravigotte to get me into bed with a man. In any event, since it's your check, I'm going to have caviar, and what English call "cutlets", and some pink champagne. I don't often date a good-looking Englishman and the dinner's going to live up to the occasion.'

They were interrupted by the arrival of the cutlets, accompanied by asparagus with mousseline sauce . . .

M smiled at him indulgently . . . 'How were the cutlets?'

'Superb,' said Bond. 'I could cut them with a fork. The best English cooking is the best in the world – particularly at this time of year.'

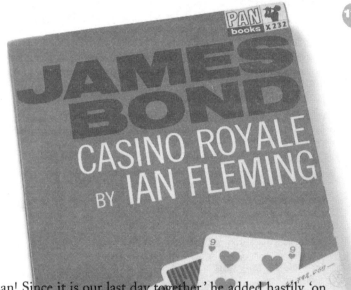

'**B**ondo-san! Since it is our last day together,' he added hastily, 'on this particular voyage, I have arranged a special treat. I ordered it by radio from the ship. A *fugu* feast!'

Bond cursed silently. The memory of his eggs Benedict the night before was intolerably sweet. What new monstrosity was this?

DINNER WITH GOLDFINGER

[From *Goldfinger*. Bond is at Goldfinger's mansion in Kent. Both are unsure as to the true intentions of the other.]

Bond lowered his paper and looked up. Goldfinger was carrying the ginger cat tucked carelessly under one arm. He reached the fireplace, bent forward and pressed the bell.

He turned towards Bond. 'Do you like cats?' His gaze was flat, incurious.

'Sufficiently.'

The service door opened. The chauffeur stood in the frame. He still wore his bowler hat and his shiny black gloves. He gazed impassively at Goldfinger. Goldfinger crooked a finger. The chauffeur approached and stood within the circle by the fire.

Goldfinger turned to Bond. He said conversationally, 'This is my handy man.' He smiled thinly. 'That is something of a joke. Oddjob, show Mr Bond your hands.' He smiled again at Bond. 'I call him Oddjob because that describes his functions on my staff.'

The Korean slowly pulled off his gloves and came and stood at arm's length from Bond and held out his hands palm upwards. Bond got up and looked at them. They were big and fat with muscle. The fingers all seemed to be the same length. They were very blunt at the tips and the tips glinted as if they were made of yellow bone.

'Turn them over and show Mr Bond the sides.'

There were no fingernails. Instead there was this same, yellowish carapace. The man turned the hands sideways. Down each edge of the hands was a hard ridge of the same bony substance.

Bond raised his eyebrows at Goldfinger.

Goldfinger said, 'We will have a demonstration.' He pointed at the thick oak banisters that ran up the stairs. The rail was a massive six inches by four thick. The Korean obediently walked over to the stairs and climbed a few steps. He stood with his hands at his sides, gazing across at Goldfinger like a good retriever. Goldfinger gave a quick nod. Impassively the Korean lifted his right hand high and straight above his head and brought the side of it down like an axe across the heavy polished rail. There was a splintering crash and the rail sagged, broken through the centre. Again the hand went up and flashed down. This time it swept right through the rail leaving a jagged gap. Splinters clattered down on to the floor of the hall. The Korean straightened himself and stood to attention, waiting for further orders. There was no flush of effort in his face and no hint of pride in his achievement.

Goldfinger beckoned. The man came back across the floor. Goldfinger said, 'His feet are the same, the outside edges of them. Oddjob, the mantelpiece.' Goldfinger pointed at the heavy shelf of carved wood above the fireplace. It was about seven feet off the ground – six inches higher than the top of the Korean's bowler hat.

'Garch a har?'

'Yes, take off your coat and hat.' Goldfinger turned to Bond. 'Poor chap's got a cleft palate. I shouldn't think there are many people who understand him besides me.'

Bond reflected how useful that would be, a slave who could only communicate with the world through his interpreter – better even than the deaf mutes of the harems, more tightly bound to his master, more secure.

Oddjob had taken off his coat and hat and placed them neatly on the floor. Now he rolled his trouser legs up to the knee and stood back in the wide well-planted stance of the judo expert. He looked as if a charging elephant wouldn't put him off balance.

'Better stand back, Mr Bond.' The teeth glittered in the wide mouth. 'This blow snaps a man's neck like a daffodil.' Goldfinger drew aside the low settee with the drink tray. Now the Korean had a clear run. But he was only three long steps away. How could he possibly reach the high mantelpiece?

Bond watched, fascinated. Now the slanting eyes in the flat yellow mask were glinting with a fierce intentness. Faced by such a man, thought Bond, one could only go down on one's knees and wait for death.

Goldfinger lifted his hand. The bunched toes in the polished soft leather shoes seemed to grip the ground. The Korean took one long crouching stride with knees well bent and then whirled off the ground. In mid-air his feet slapped together like a ballet dancer's, but higher than a ballet dancer's have ever reached, and then the body bent sideways and downwards and the right foot shot out like a piston. There came a crashing thud. Gracefully the body settled back down on the hands, now splayed on the floor, the elbows bent to take the weight and then straightened sharply to throw the man up and back on his feet.

Oddjob stood to attention. This time there was a gleam of triumph in his flat eyes as he looked at the three-inch jagged bite the edge of his foot had taken out of the mantelpiece.

Bond looked at the man in deep awe. And only two nights ago, he, Bond, had been working on his manual of unarmed combat! There was nothing, absolutely nothing, in all his reading, all his experience, to approach what he had just witnessed. This was not a man of flesh and blood. This was a living club, perhaps the most dangerous animal on the face of the earth. Bond had to do it, had to give homage to this uniquely dreadful person. He held out his hand.

'Softly, Oddjob.' Goldfinger's voice was the crack of a whip.

The Korean bowed his head and took Bond's hand in his. He kept his fingers straight and merely bent his thumb in a light clasp. It was like holding a piece of board. He released Bond's hand and went to his neat pile of clothes.

'Forgive me, Mr Bond, and I appreciate your gesture.' Goldfinger's face showed his approval. 'But Oddjob doesn't know his own strength – particularly when he is keyed up. And those hands are like machine-tools. He could have crushed your hand to pulp without meaning to. Now then,' Oddjob had dressed and was standing respectfully at attention, 'you did well, Oddjob. I'm glad to see you are in training. Here –' Goldfinger took the cat from under his arm and tossed it to the Korean who caught it eagerly – 'I am tired of seeing this animal around. You may have it for dinner.' The Korean's eyes gleamed. 'And tell them in the kitchen that we will have our own dinner at once.'

The Korean inclined his head sharply and turned away.

Bond hid his disgust. He realized that all this exhibition was simply a message to him, a warning, a light rap on the knuckles. It said, 'You see my power, Mr Bond. I could easily have killed you or maimed you. Oddjob was giving an exhibition and you got in the way. I would certainly be innocent and Oddjob would get off with a light sentence. Instead, the cat will be punished in your place. Bad luck on the cat, of course.'

Bond said casually, 'Why does the man always wear that bowler hat?'

'Oddjob.' The Korean had reached the service door. 'The hat.' Goldfinger pointed at a panel in the woodwork near the fireplace.

Still holding the cat under his left arm, Oddjob turned and walked stolidly back towards them. When he was halfway across the floor, and without pausing or taking aim, he reached up to his hat, took it by the rim and flung it sideways with all his force. There was a loud clang. For an instant the rim of the bowler hat stuck an inch deep in the panel Goldfinger had indicated, then it fell and clattered on the floor.

Goldfinger smiled politely at Bond. 'A light but very strong alloy, Mr Bond. I fear that will have damaged the felt covering, but Odd-job will put on another. He's surprisingly quick with a needle and thread. As you can imagine, that blow would have smashed a man's skull or half severed his neck. A homely and most ingenious con-cealed weapon, I'm sure you will agree.'

'Yes, indeed.' Bond smiled with equal politeness. 'Useful chap to have around.'

Oddjob had picked up his hat and disappeared. There came the boom of a gong. 'Ah, dinner! Shall we go in?'

MAN TALK
'I used to throw scraps to her under the table'

'But did I talk a lot of crap last night? Or did you? Seem to recollect that one of us did.'

'You only gave me hell about the state of the world and called me a poofter. But you were quite friendly about it. No offence given or taken.'

'Oh, Christ!' Dikko Henderson gloomily pushed a hand through his tough, grizzled hair. 'But I didn't hit anyone?'

'Only that girl you slapped so hard on the bottom that she fell down.'

Bond had never killed in cold blood, and he hadn't liked watching, and helping, someone else do it ... Kerim seemed to sense Bond's thoughts. 'Life is full of death, my friend,' he said philosophically.

On their way home Leiter asked a string of questions about Solitaire. Finally he said casually: 'By the way, hope I fixed the rooms like you wanted them.'

'Couldn't be better,' said Bond cheerfully.

'Fine,' said Leiter. 'Just occurred to me you two might be hyphenating.'

‘That girl may be your fiancée or she may not [said Scaramanga], but that ploy with the shower bath. That's an old hood's trick. Probably a Secret Service one too. Unless, that is, you were screwin' her.' He raised one eyebrow.

'I was. Anything wrong with that? What have you been doing with the Chinese girl? Playing mahjongg?'

'**007**? Meet No. 000.'

Bond swung round. It was! It was Felix Leiter!

Leiter, his CIA companion on some of the most thrilling cases in Bond's career, grinned and thrust the steel hook that was his right hand under Bond's arm. 'Take it easy, friend. Dick Tracy will tell all when we get out of here. Bags are out front. Let's go.'

Bond said, 'Well, God damn it! You old so-and-so! Did you know it was going to be me?'

'Sure. CIA knows all.'

[Leiter] banked the little plane sharply. 'But you see what I mean? If that little heap of ironmongery isn't worth a quarter of a billion dollars my name's P. Rick.'

'But don't think you can ask for a lawyer or the British Consul if you get in bad with the Mob. Only law firm out there's called Smith and Wesson.' He banged on the table with his hook. 'Better have one last Bourbon and branch-water.'

Bond had a natural affection for coloured people, but he reflected how lucky England was compared with America where you had to live with the colour problem from your schooldays up. He smiled as he remembered something Felix Leiter had said to him on their last assignment together in America. Bond had referred to Mr Big, the famous Harlem criminal, as 'that damned nigger'. Leiter had picked him up. 'Careful now, James,' he had said. 'People are so dam' sensitive about colour around here that you can't even ask a barman for a jigger of rum. You have to ask for a jegro.'

'**W**hew!' Bond mopped his brow. 'Remember that Moonraker job I was on a few years back? Interesting to see what the people out front saw.'

'Yeah. You were lucky to get out of that deep fry.' Leiter brushed aside Bond's reminiscences.

A girl, sunbathing naked on the roof of a smart cabin cruiser, hastily snatched at a towel.

'Authentic blonde!' commented Leiter.

James Bond looked Major Smythe squarely in the eyes. 'It just happened that Oberhauser was a friend of mine. He taught me to ski before the war, when I was in my teens. He was a wonderful man. He was something of a father to me at a time when I happened to need one.'

'I may be able to help,' said Leiter. 'I was a regular in our Marine Corps before I joined this racket, if that means anything to you.' He looked at Bond with a hint of self-deprecation.

'It does,' said Bond.

'I had a little Bessarabian hell-cat [said Kerim]. I had won her in a fight with some gypsies, here in the hills of Istanbul. They came after me, but I got her on board the boat. I had to knock her unconscious first. She was still trying to kill me when we got back to Trebizond, so I got her to my place and took away all her clothes and kept her chained naked under the table. When I ate, I used to throw scraps to her under the table, like a dog. She had to learn who was master. Before that could happen my mother did an unheard of thing. She visited my place without warning. She came to tell me that my father wanted to see me immediately. She found the girl. My mother was really angry with me for the first time in my life. Angry? She was beside herself. I was a cruel ne'er-do-well and she was ashamed to call me her son. The girl must immediately be taken back to her people. My mother brought her some of her own clothes from the house. The girl put them on, but when the time came, she refused to leave me.' Darko Kerim laughed hugely. 'An interesting lesson in female psychology, my dear friend.'

'You still got that double o number that means you're allowed to kill?'

'Yes,' said Bond dryly. 'I have.'

This was Quarrel, the Cayman Islander, and Bond liked him immediately. There was the blood of Cromwellian soldiers and buccaneers in him and his face was strong and angular and his mouth was almost severe. His eyes were grey. It was only the spatulate nose and the pale palms of his hands that were negroid.

Bond shook him by the hand.

'Good morning, Captain,' said Quarrel. Coming from the most famous race of seamen in the world, this was the highest title he knew. But there was no desire to please, or humility, in his voice. He was speaking as mate of the ship and his manner was straightforward and candid.

That moment defined their relationship. It remained that of a Scots laird with his head stalker; authority was unspoken and there was no room for servility.

The huge right fist crashed into the left palm with the noise of a .45 pistol shot. The great square face of the Australian turned almost purple and the veins stood out on the grizzled temples . . .

'For God's sake, Dikko! How in hell did we get on to politics? Let's go and get some food. I'll agree there's a certain aboriginal common sense in what you say . . .'

'Don't talk to me about the aborigines! What in hell do you think you know about the aborigines? Do you know that in my country there's a move afoot, not afoot, at full gallop, to give the aborigines the vote? You pommy poofter. You give me any more of that liberal crap and I'll have your balls for a bow-tie.'

NATURE NOTES

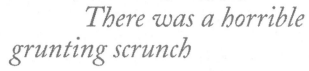

There was a horrible grunting scrunch

The octopus explored his right hand with its buccal orifice and took a first tentative bite at a finger with its beak-like jaws.

Inside, Bond's torch shone everywhere into red eyes that glowed like rubies in the darkness and there was a soft movement and a scuttling. He sprayed the light up and down the fuselage. Everywhere there were octopuses, small ones, but perhaps a hundred of them, weaving on the tips of their tentacles, sliding softly away into protecting shadows, changing their camouflage nervously from brown to pale phosphorescence that gleamed palely in the patches of darkness. The whole fuselage seemed to be crawling with them, evilly, horribly, and as Bond shone his torch on the roof the sight was even worse. There, bumping softly in the slight current, hung the corpse of a crew member. In decomposition, it had risen up from the floor, and octopuses, hanging from it like bats, now let go their hold and shot, jet propelled, to and fro inside the plane – dreadful, glinting, red-eyed comets that slapped themselves into dark corners and stealthily squeezed themselves into cracks and under seats.

Bond closed his mind to the disgusting nightmare and, weaving his torch in front of him, proceeded with his search.

For a moment blind rage seized him. He kicked out sharply, twice. One short scream came up out of the depths. There was a splash and then a great commotion in the water.

Bond walked to the side of the trap-door and pushed the upright concrete slab. It revolved easily on its central pivot.

Just before its edges shut out the blackness below, Bond heard one terrible snuffling grunt as if a great pig was getting its mouth full. He knew it for the grunt that a shark makes as its hideous flat nose comes up out of the water and its sickle-shaped mouth closes on a floating carcass. He shuddered and kicked the bolt home with his foot.

Out of range of Bond's light there was a steady, quiet, scuttling sound, and in the blackness hundreds of pinpoints of red light flickered and moved. It was the same uphill and downhill. Twenty yards away on either side, a thousand rats were looking at Bond. They were sniffing at his scent. Bond imagined the whiskers lifting slightly from their teeth. He had a quick moment of wondering what action they would take if his torch went out.

The sting-ray was about six feet from wing-tip to wing-tip, and perhaps ten feet long from the blunt wedge of its nose to the end of its deadly tail. It was dark grey with that violet tinge that is so often a danger signal in the underwater world. When it rose up from the pale golden sand and swam a little distance it was as if a black towel was being waved through the water.

Now suddenly the alarm was sounded by a hidden nerve – Danger! Danger! Danger!

Bond's body tensed. His hand went to his knife and his head swivelled sharply to the right – not to the left or behind him. His senses told him to look to the right.

A big barracuda, if it is twenty pounds or over, is the most fearsome fish in the seas. Clean and straight and malevolent, it is all hostile weapon from the long snarling mouth in the cruel jaw that can open like a rattlesnake's to an angle of ninety degrees, along the blue and silver steel of the body to the lazy power of the tail-fin that helps to make this fish one of the five fastest sprinters in the seas. This one, moving parallel with Bond, ten yards away just inside the wall of grey mist that was the edge of visibility, was showing its danger signals. The broad lateral stripes showed vividly – the angry hunting signal – the gold and black tiger's eye was on him, watchful, incurious, and the long mouth was open half an inch so that the moonlight glittered on the sharpest row of teeth in the ocean – teeth that don't bite at the flesh, teeth that tear out a chunk and swallow and then hit and scythe again.

Bond's stomach crawled with the ants of fear and his skin tightened at his groin.

Then, blood pouring from his bitten lower lip, he bent carefully down to look into Octopussy's house. Yes! the brown mass was still there. It was stirring excitedly. Why? Major Smythe saw the dark strings of his blood curling lazily down through the water. Of course! The darling was tasting his blood.

He shivered at the prospect of the dark adventure under the sea that he had already put off in his mind until tomorrow. Suddenly he loathed and feared the sea and everything in it. The millions of tiny antennae that would stare and point as he went by that night, the eyes that would wake and watch him, the pulses that would miss for the hundredth of a second and then go beating quietly on, the jelly tendrils that would grope and reach for him, as blind in the light as in the dark.

'Ever seen a man that's stepped on a stone-fish? His body bends backwards like a bow with the pain. Sometimes it's so frightful his eyes literally fall out of their sockets. They very seldom live.'

Once, something slithered away from his approaching feet and disappeared with a heavy rustle into the fallen leaves under a tree. What snakes were there that really went for a man? The king-cobra, black mamba, the saw-scaled viper, the rattlesnake and the fer-de-lance.

That night Bond's dreams were full of terrifying encounters with giant squids and sting-rays, hammerheads and the saw-teeth of barracuda, so that he whimpered and sweated in his sleep.

Doctor No sat back in his chair. His eyes were now fixed on the girl, watching her reactions. She stared back at him, half hypnotized, like a bush mouse in front of a rattlesnake . . .

'You are a Jamaican, so you will know what I am talking about. This island is called Crab Key. It is called by that name because it is infested with crabs, land crabs – what they call in Jamaica "black crabs". You know them. They weigh about a pound each and they are as big as saucers. At this time of year they come up in thousands from their holes near the shore and climb up towards the mountain. There, in the coral uplands, they go to ground again in holes in the rock and spawn their broods. They march up in armies of hundreds at a time. They march through everything and over everything. In Jamaica they go through houses that are in their path. They are like the lemmings of Norway. It is a compulsive migration.' Doctor No paused. He said softly, 'But there is a difference. The crabs devour what they find in their path. And at present, woman, they are "running". They are coming up the mountainside in their tens of thousands, great red and orange and black waves of them, scuttling and hurrying and scraping against the rock above us at this moment. And tonight, in the middle of their path, they are going to find the naked body of a woman pegged out – a banquet spread for them – and they will feel the warm body with their feeding pincers, and one will make the first incision with his fighting claws and then . . . and then . . .'

There was a moan from the girl. Her head fell forward slackly on to her chest. She had fainted.

He risked a quick glance with his pencil torch and immediately the underbelly of the mass of brown tree-coral came alive. Anemones with crimson centres waved their velvet tentacles at him, a colony of black sea-eggs moved their toledo-steel spines in sudden alarm and a hairy sea-centipede halted in its hundred strides and questioned with its eyeless head.

Bond said, 'What should I expect to see at this time of night? Any big fish about?'

Santos grinned. 'Usual harbour stuff, sah. Some barracuda perhaps. Mebbe a shark. But they's lazy an overfed with the refuse and muck from de drains. Dey won't trouble you – less you bleedin' that is. They'll be night-crawlin' things on the bottom – lobster, crab, mebbe a small pus-feller or two.'

It was while he was measuring the dangers ahead that the octopus got him. Round both ankles.

'**A**nd you have of course heard of the South American piranha fish? They can strip a whole horse to the bones in less than an hour. The scientific name is Serrasalmus. The sub-species Nattereri is the most voracious. Our good doctor has preferred these fish to our native goldfish for his lakes.'

Once, out of the corner of his eye, he saw a sting-ray as big as a ping-pong table shuffle out of his path, the tip of its great speckled wings beating like a bird's, its long horned tail streaming out behind it.

Then the shark's snout came right out of the water and it drove in towards the head, the lower curved jaw open so that light glinted on the teeth. There was a horrible grunting scrunch and a great swirl of water. Then silence.

Bond inched forward, the lighter held before him. It was some sort of a cage with small things living in it. He could hear them scuttling back, away from the light. A foot away from the mesh he dowsed the light and waited for his eyes to get used to the dark. As he waited, listening, he could hear the tiny scuttling back towards him, and gradually the forest of red pinpoints gathered again, peering at him through the mesh.

What was it? Bond listened to the pounding of his heart. Snakes? Scorpions? Centipedes?

Carefully he brought his eyes close up to the little glowing forest. He inched the lighter up beside his face and suddenly pressed the lever. He caught a glimpse of tiny claws hooked through the mesh and of dozens of thick furry feet and of furry sacklike stomachs topped by big insect heads that seemed to be covered with eyes . . .

Often in the shadows there were unexplained, heavy movements and swirls in the water and the sudden glare of large eyes at once extinguished.

Below him the water quivered. Something was stirring in the depths, something huge. A great length of luminescent greyness showed, poised far down in the darkness. Something snaked up from it, a whiplash as thick as Bond's arm . . . What was it doing? Was it . . . ? Was it tasting the blood?

As if in answer, two eyes as big as footballs slowly swam up and into Bond's vision. They stopped, twenty feet below his own, and stared up through the quiet water at his face.

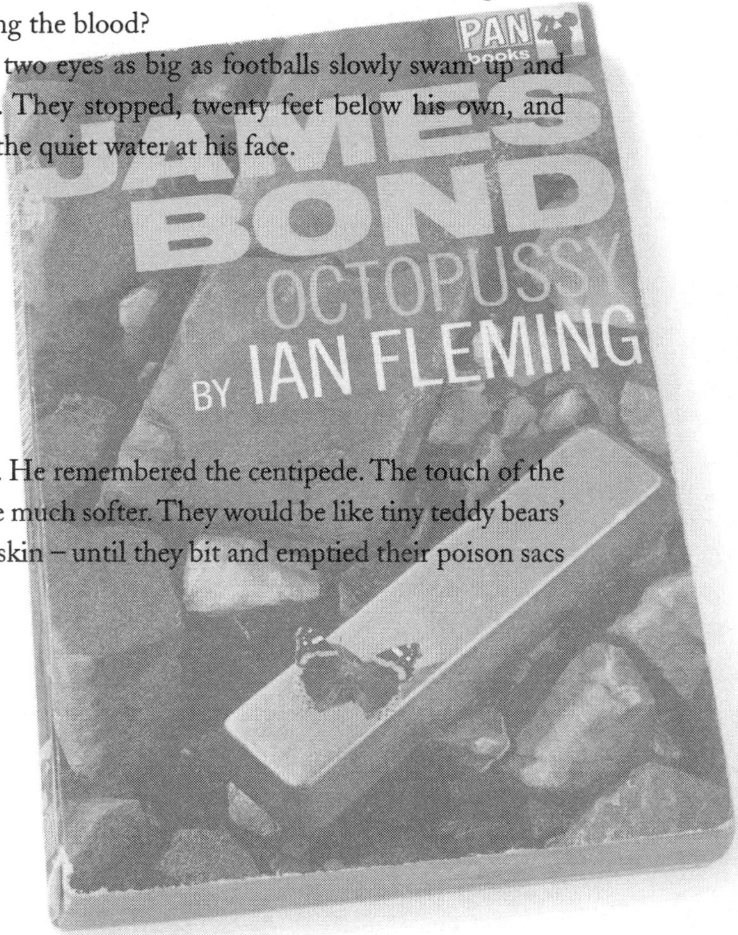

Bond shuddered. He remembered the centipede. The touch of the tarantulas would be much softer. They would be like tiny teddy bears' paws against one's skin – until they bit and emptied their poison sacs into you.

DREADFUL EVENTS
'Prepare the blowlamp and
the electrical machine'

What a shambles! The place looked like a butcher's shop. How much blood did a body contain? He remembered. Ten pints. Well, it would soon all be there.

Flames started to bleed slowly from the chromium mouth of the car. Someone was scrabbling at a window, trying to get out. At any moment the flames would find the vacuum pump and run the whole length of the chassis to the tank. And then it would be too late.

It was the deadly hand-edge blow to the Adam's apple, delivered with the fingers locked into a blade, that had been the standby of the Commandos. If the Mexican was still alive, he was certainly dead before he hit the ground.

There was an obscene smell of high explosive, of burning wood, and of, yes, that was it – roast mutton.

When they were both tied securely and painfully to the arms and legs of two tubular steel chairs a few feet apart beneath the glass wall-map, Krebs left the room. He came back in a moment with a mechanic's blowtorch.

He set the ugly machine on the desk, pumped air into it with a few brisk strokes of the plunger, and set a match to it. A blue flame hissed out a couple of inches into the room. He picked up the instrument and walked towards Gala. He stopped a few feet to one side of her.

'Now then,' said Drax grimly. 'Let's get this over without any fuss. The good Krebs is an artist with one of those things. We used to call him *Der Zwangsmann* – the Persuader. I shall never forget the way he went over the last spy we caught together. Just south of the Rhine, wasn't it, Krebs?'

Bond pricked up his ears.

'Yes, *mein Kapitän*.' Krebs chuckled reminiscently. 'It was a pig of a Belgian.'

'All right, then,' said Drax. 'Just remember, you two. There's no fair play down here. No jolly good sports and all that. This is business.' The voice cracked like a whip on the word.

The man's face hit the table top with a thud, bounced up, and half turned towards Bond. Bond's right flashed out and the face of the Rolex disintegrated against the man's jaw. The body slid sluggishly off its chair on to the carpet and lay still, its legs untidy as if in sleep. The eyes fluttered and stared, unseeing, upwards. Bond went round the desk and bent down. There was no heartbeat.

'Next day some innocent guy is driving into town from Boulder City, and he spots something pink sticking up out of the desert. Couldn't be a cactus or anything, so he stops and has himself a look.' Leiter prodded Bond's chest with a finger. 'My friend, that pink thing sticking up was an arm. And the hand at the top of the arm was holding a full deck of cards, fanned out. The cops came with spades and dug around and there was the rest of the guy under the ground at the other end of the arm. That was the dealer. They'd blown the back of his head off and buried him. The fancy work with the arm and the cards was just to warn the others. Now how d'ya like that?'

'Not bad,' said Bond.

Blofeld spoke from the other end of the room. He spoke in English. He said, in a loud voice that boomed around the naked walls, 'Commander Bond, or number 007 in the British Secret Service if you prefer it, this is the Question Room, a device of my invention that has the almost inevitable effect of making silent people talk. As you know, this property is highly volcanic. You are now sitting directly above a geyser that throws mud, at a heat of around one thousand degrees Centigrade, a distance of approximately one hundred feet into the air. Your body is now at an elevation of approximately fifty feet directly above its source. I had the whimsical notion to canalize this geyser up a stone funnel above which you now sit. This is what is known as a periodic geyser. This particular example is regulated to erupt volcanically on exactly each fifteenth minute in every hour.' Blofeld looked behind him and turned back. 'You will therefore observe that you have exactly eleven minutes before the next eruption.'

The great pack of barracudas seemed to have gone mad. They were whirling and snapping in the water like hysterical dogs. Three sharks that had joined them were charging through the water with a clumsier frenzy. The water was boiling with the dreadful fish and Bond was slammed in the face and buffeted again and again within a few yards. At any moment he knew his rubber skin would be torn with the flesh below it and then the pack would be on him . . .

. . . He looked up and saw with dawning comprehension that the quicksilver surface of the sea had turned red, a horrible glinting crimson.

Threads of the stuff drifted within his reach. He hooked some towards him with the end of his gun. Held the end close up against his glass mask.

There was no doubt about it.

Up above, someone was spraying the surface of the sea with blood and offal.

The head jerked back. For an instant, steel-capped teeth showed in the gaping mouth. Then the grey Homburg fell off and the dead head slumped.

As he did so, there came a terrible scream from behind him, a loud splintering of wood, and the screech of the train's brakes being applied.

At the same time, the spray from the snow-fan, that had now reached Bond, turned pink!

The big man stood for a moment and looked up at the deep blue sky. His fingers opened in a spasm and let go the knife. His pierced heart stuttered and limped and stopped. He crashed flat back and lay, his arms flung wide, as if someone had thrown him away.

He waited for his breath to calm down and then slipped back his cowl and listened. Not a wisp of wind stirred in the trees, but from somewhere came the sound of softly running water and, in the background, a regular, glutinous burping and bubbling. The fumaroles!

For the first time in his life, Bond went berserk . . . The pressure of the hands on Bond's throat slackened. The hands fell away. Now the tongue came out and lolled from the open mouth and there came a terrible gargling from deep in the lungs. Bond sat astride the silent chest and slowly, one by one, unhinged his rigid fingers.

Blofeld pointed to the pile of Bond's possessions on the floor. 'Kono, take those away. I will examine them later. And you can wait with the guards in the outer hall. Prepare the blowlamp and the electrical machine for further examination in case it should be necessary.' He turned to Bond. 'And now – talk and you will receive an honourable and quick death by the sword.'

But then the Colt spoke its single word, and the killer and [motor-cycle], as if lassoed from within the forest, veered crazily off the road, leapt the ditch and crashed head-on into the trunk of a beech. For a moment the tangle of man and machinery clung to the broad trunk and then, with a metallic death-rattle, toppled backwards into the grass.

Bond got off his machine and walked over to the ugly twist of khaki and smoking steel. There was no need to feel for a pulse. Wherever the bullet had struck, the crash helmet had smashed like an eggshell.

'**I**s that your last word?' His right hand went behind his back and he clicked his fingers softly, once. Behind him the gun-hands of the two men slid through the opening of their gay shirts above the waistbands. The sharp animal eyes watched the Major's fingers behind his back . . .

The fingers clicked. Major Gonzales stepped to one side to give a clear field of fire. The brown monkey-hands came out from under the gay shirts. The ugly sausage-shaped hunks of metal spat and thudded – again and again, even when the two bodies were on their way to the ground.

The quality of the scream had been of sudden, fully realized terror as the man fell, scrabbled at the ice with his finger-nails and boots, and then, as he gathered speed down the polished blue gully, the blinding horror of the truth. And what a death!

The negro was bent double, his hands between his legs, uttering little panting screams. Bond whipped the gun down hard on the back of the woolly skull. It gave back a dull klonk as if he had hammered on a door . . .

It was perhaps five minutes later when a tiny movement of the air against his face made Bond open his eyes. In front of his eyes was a hand, a man's hand, reaching softly for the lever of the accelerator [on the traction machine]. Bond watched it, at first fascinated, and then with dawning horror as the lever was slowly depressed and the straps began to haul madly at his body. He shouted – something, he didn't know what. His whole body was racked with a great pain. Desperately he lifted his head and shouted again. On the dial, the needle was trembling at 200! His head dropped back, exhausted. Through a mist of sweat he watched the hand softly release the lever. The hand paused and turned slowly so that the back of the wrist was just below his eyes. In the centre of the wrist was the little red sign of the zigzag and the two bisecting lines. A voice said quietly, close up against his ear, 'You will not meddle again, my friend'. Then there was nothing but the great whine and groan of the machine and the bite of the straps that were tearing his body in half. Bond began to scream, weakly, while the sweat poured from him and dripped off the leather cushions on to the floor.

Bond had taken out the Walther PPK. He checked to see there was a round in the chamber, rested it on his left forearm and waited for the two sharks to come round again. The first was the bigger, a hammerhead nearly twelve foot long. Its hideously distorted head moved slowly from side to side as it nuzzled through the water, watching what went on below, waiting for the sign of meat. Bond aimed for the base of the dorsal fin that cut through the water like a dark sail. It was fully erect, a sign of tension and awareness in the big fish. Just below it was the spine, unassailable except with a nickel-plated bullet. He pulled the trigger. There was a phut as the bullet hit the surface just behind the dorsal. The boom of the heavy gun rolled away over the sea. The shark paid no attention. Bond fired again. The water foamed as the fish reared itself above the surface, dived shallowly and came up thrashing sideways like a broken snake. It was a brief flurry ... [The following shark] made a short snapping run and swerved away. Feeling safe, it darted in again, seemed to nuzzle at the dying fish and then lifted its snout above the surface and came down with all its force, scything into the flank of the hammerhead. It got hold, but the flesh was tough. It shook its great brown head like a dog, worrying at the mouthful, and then tore itself away. A cloud of blood poured over the sea. Now another shark appeared from below and both fish, in a frenzy tore and tore again at the still moving hulk whose nervous system refused to die.

The dreadful feast moved away on the current and was soon only a distant splashing on the surface of the quiet sea.

Mr Big looked across at Bond.

'Which finger do you use least, Mister Bond?'

Bond was startled by the question. His mind raced.

'On reflection, I expect you will say the little finger of the left hand,' continued the soft voice. 'Tee-Hee, break the little finger of Mr Bond's left hand.'

142

When, dazed and half-conscious, he raised himself on one knee, a ghastly rain of pieces of flesh and shreds of blood-soaked clothing fell on him and around him, mingled with branches and gravel.

Blofeld looked down the table. His eyes were fixed on the man standing – on No. 7. The Corsican, Marius Domingue, looked back at him steadily. He knew he was innocent. His body was still with tension. But it was not fear. He had faith, as they all had, in the rightness of Blofeld. He could not understand why he had been singled out as a target for all the eyes that were now upon him, but Blofeld had decided, and Blofeld was always right.

Blofeld noticed the man's courage and sensed the reasons for it. He also observed the sweat shining on the face of No. 12, the man alone at the head of the table. Good! The sweat would improve the contact.

Under the table, Blofeld's right hand came up off his thigh, found the knob, and pulled the switch.

The body of Pierre Borraud, seized in the iron fist of 3,000 volts, arced in the armchair as if it had been kicked in the back. The rough mat of black hair rose sharply straight up on his head and remained upright, a gollywog fringe for the contorted, bursting face. The eyes glared wildly and then faded. A blackened tongue slowly protruded between the snarling teeth and remained hideously extended. Thin wisps of smoke rose from under the hands, from the middle of the back, and from under the thighs where the concealed electrodes in the chair had made contact. Blofeld pulled the switch. The lights in the room that had dimmed to orange, making a dull supernatural glow, brightened to normal. The roasted meat and burned fabric smell spread slowly. The body of No. 12 crumpled horribly. There was a sharp crack as the chin hit the edge of the table. It was all over . . . Now, the members, ignoring the heap of death at the end of the table, settled in their chairs. It was time to get back to business.

KEY TO
QUOTATIONS

16
You Only Live Twice
From Russia with Love

17
Dr No
Live and Let Die
From Russia with Love

18
Goldfinger
From Russia with Love

19
Live and Let Die

20
You Only Live Twice
On Her Majesty's Secret
  Service
Moonraker

21
Dr No
From Russia with Love
For Your Eyes Only

22
Live and Let Die
Thunderball

23
Goldfinger
You Only Live Twice

24
Dr No

25
Thunderball

26
Casino Royale
Dr No
Moonraker
Live and Let Die

27
You Only Live Twice
Thunderball
You Only Live Twice

28
Goldfinger
The Man with the Golden
  Gun

29
On Her Majesty's Secret
  Service
Casino Royale
Moonraker

30
Moonraker

31
From Russia with Love
The Spy Who Loved Me

32
Thunderball
Diamonds are Forever
The Spy Who Loved Me

33
Casino Royale
Goldfinger

34
Goldfinger
Diamonds are Forever

35
Dr No
From Russia with Love
On Her Majesty's Secret
  Service

36
Diamonds are Forever
From Russia with Love

37
Octopussy
Live and Let Die

38
Casino Royale
Live and Let Die
The Spy Who Loved Me
Moonraker
Moonraker

39
Diamonds are Forever
The Spy Who Loved Me

40
Diamonds are Forever

45
Moonraker
From Russia with Love

46
You Only Live Twice
Casino Royale

47
Casino Royale
Octopussy
Octopussy

48
Live and Let Die
*The Man with the Golden
   Gun*

49
Goldfinger
Diamonds are Forever
Goldfinger
*On Her Majesty's Secret
   Service*

50
Dr No

51
Dr No
For Your Eyes Only

52
Moonraker
Thunderball
Goldfinger

53
Live and Let Die
Moonraker
Moonraker

54
Live and Let Die
Goldfinger
Moonraker
From Russia with Love

55
Diamonds are Forever
Goldfinger

56
*The Man with the Golden
   Gun*
Thunderball
Moonraker
Thunderball

57
Diamonds are Forever
You Only Live Twice
Goldfinger
Diamonds are Forever

58
Goldfinger
Diamonds are Forever
*On Her Majesty's Secret
   Service*
For Your Eyes Only

59
Dr No

60
Goldfinger
For Your Eyes Only
*On Her Majesty's Secret
   Service*
Goldfinger

61
Thunderball

62
Moonraker
Dr No
Thunderball
From Russia with Love

63
Diamonds are Forever
Diamonds are Forever
Thunderball
*On Her Majesty's Secret
   Service*

64
*The Man with the Golden
   Gun*
*The Man with the Golden
   Gun*

69
Moonraker
Diamonds are Forever
From Russia with Love
From Russia with Love

70
You Only Live Twice
For Your Eyes Only
Casino Royale
Casino Royale

71
For Your Eyes Only
Casino Royale
For Your Eyes Only
You Only Live Twice
Goldfinger

72
Live and Let Die
Goldfinger
From Russia with Love
Diamonds are Forever

73
The Spy Who Loved Me
Live and Let Die
Diamonds are Forever

74
You Only Live Twice
Live and Let Die
From Russia with Love
You Only Live Twice

75
From Russia with Love
Casino Royale

76
Dr No
Moonraker
Goldfinger

77
From Russia with Love
From Russia with Love
Dr No
*On Her Majesty's Secret
    Service*
*On Her Majesty's Secret
    Service*

78
Diamonds are Forever
Dr No
Goldfinger
Live and Let Die

79
From Russia with Love
Casino Royale
*On Her Majesty's Secret
    Service*
Goldfinger
Casino Royale

80
Casino Royale
Diamonds are Forever
Thunderball
Casino Royale
Goldfinger

81
Diamonds are Forever
Goldfinger
Casino Royale
Live and Let Die

82
Casino Royale
Diamonds are Forever
For Your Eyes Only

83
Casino Royale
Goldfinger
Diamonds are Forever

84
Thunderball
*On Her Majesty's Secret
    Service*

85
*On Her Majesty's Secret
    Service*
Goldfinger

86
Live and Let Die
Moonraker

87
Moonraker

91
Casino Royale
Live and Let Die
Goldfinger

92
Diamonds are Forever
Goldfinger
Casino Royale
Goldfinger

93
Moonraker

94
Diamonds are Forever
Diamonds are Forever
You Only Live Twice
Live and Let Die

95
Live and Let Die
Moonraker
Diamonds are Forever

96
For Your Eyes Only
Diamonds are Forever
Casino Royale

97
Thunderball
Octopussy
Dr No
Octopussy

98
On Her Majesty's Secret
Service
Moonraker
On Her Majesty's Secret
Service
Moonraker
Moonraker

99
On Her Majesty's Secret
Service
Dr No
Dr No
On Her Majesty's Secret
Service

100
Live and Let Die
Moonraker
For Your Eyes Only
You Only Live Twice

101
Moonraker
You Only Live Twice
From Russia with Love

102
You Only Live Twice
You Only Live Twice
Goldfinger
The Man with the Golden
Gun
Dr No

103
Thunderball
Thunderball
Casino Royale

104
The Spy Who Loved Me
Thunderball

105
Casino Royale
From Russia with Love
You Only Live Twice

106
Casino Royale
Casino Royale
Live and Let Die
From Russia with Love

107
Thunderball
On Her Majesty's Secret
Service
Casino Royale

108
Dr No
From Russia with Love
Dr No
For Your Eyes Only

109
Casino Royale
Live and Let Die
Live and Let Die

110
Live and Let Die
Live and Let Die
Live and Let Die
Goldfinger

111
Goldfinger
Goldfinger

112

*The Man with the Golden
    Gun*
Moonraker
You Only Live Twice

113

From Russia with Love
From Russia with Love

114

Moonraker
You Only Live Twice
Diamonds are Forever
Diamonds are Forever

115

Diamonds are Forever
Moonraker
You Only Live Twice

121

You Only Live Twice
From Russia with Love
Live and Let Die

122

*The Man with the Golden
    Gun*
Thunderball
Thunderball
Diamonds are Forever

123

Diamonds are Forever
Thunderball
Thunderball
Octopussy

124

Casino Royale
From Russia with Love
Diamonds are Forever

125

Live and Let Die
You Only Live Twice

126

Octopussy
Thunderball

127

Live and Let Die
From Russia with Love
For Your Eyes Only

128

Thunderball
Octopussy

129

Live and Let Die
For Your Eyes Only
You Only Live Twice
Live and Let Die

130

Dr No

131

Live and Let Die
Thunderball
Live and Let Die
You Only Live Twice

132

Live and Let Die
Live and Let Die
Dr No

133

Live and Let Die
Dr No
Dr No

134

From Russia with Love
Diamonds are Forever
Goldfinger
Casino Royale

135

Moonraker
*On Her Majesty's Secret
    Service*

136

Diamonds are Forever
You Only Live Twice

137

Live and Let Die
*The Man with the Golden
    Gun*
*On Her Majesty's Secret
    Service*

138

*The Man with the Golden
    Gun*
You Only Live Twice
Goldfinger
You Only Live Twice

149

CASINO ROYALE / IAN FLEMING

LIVE AND LET DIE / FLEMI

MOONRAKER / IAN FLEMING

DIAMONDS ARE FOREVER / FL

FROM RUSSIA, WITH LOVE / FLE

Dr. NO / IAN FLEMING

GOLDFINGER / IAN FLEMI